The Poe Papers

The Poe Papers

A TALE OF PASSION

NANCY ZAROULIS

PEGASUS BOOKS
NEW YORK

THE POE PAPERS

Pegasus Books LLC
45 Wall Street, Suite 1021
New York, NY 10005

First Pegasus Books edition 2007

Library of Congress Cataloging-in-Publication Data is available.

ISBN: 978-1-933648-64-4

10 9 8 7 8 6 5 4 3 2 1

Printed in the United States of America
Distributed by Consortium

The historian, essentially, wants more documents than he can really use; the dramatist only wants more liberties than he can really take.

Henry James
Preface to *The Aspern Papers*

For William Targ

Brilliant Editor, kind friend,
devoted husband to his beloved Roslyn,
much-missed Gentleman of the Old School

Author's Note

In 1848, Edgar Allan Poe traveled to Lowell, Massachusetts, to lecture on American poets and poetry. While he was there, he met a young, attractive woman, Mrs. Charles Richmond. They fell in love; they corresponded. Poe wrote "For Annie" for Mrs. Richmond; she also appears in "Landor's Cottage."

In 1849, Poe died. Mrs. Richmond lived until 1898. People often asked her for permission to see Poe's letters, but she never allowed anyone to look at them. Occasionally she would copy portions of them for scholars. She destroyed them before she died.

From these facts I constructed *The Poe Papers*, as Henry James constructed *The Aspern Papers* from the facts of Lord Byron's affair with Claire Clairmont. As far as I know, Mrs. Richmond was never troubled by so persistent a treasure hunter as I have imagined, although she must have been severely pressed from time to time. There is a rumor of complete copies of the letters having been made, which themselves mysteriously disappeared. Who made them? When? How? We don't know. But the passions of the dedicated connoisseur run strong and deep, and so it was not difficult to imagine a gentleman traveling to Lowell one day in hot pursuit of a rumored cache of priceless papers, willing to do almost anything to get them. . . .

The Poe Papers

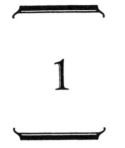

1

Lowell
January 20, 1895

SEVERAL TIMES during the interminable journey from Boston I reminded myself that the great thing was to make her understand me. Do that, I thought, and inevitably I must succeed. I would get from her what I so desperately wanted. Armed as I was with only her address and a few tantalizing facts—the meager extent of my informant's knowledge—I needed all my courage to sustain me. I was nothing—no one—to her; and she, until two weeks previous, had been nothing to me for I had assumed that she had died years ago. To learn that she lived still had been a terrible shock from which I had not recovered for several days. Then, of course, it had become clear at once what I must do: I must see her, speak to her, convince her of my worth—I must, in fact, incarcerate myself in the crowded, smelly railway carriage where I now sat; I must endure the journey to the city where she made her home. Somehow I

11

must persuade her to grant me an audience. Perched on my uncomfortable seat, I watched the snow-covered countryside through which we made our noisy, dirty way. Its sharp black-on-white was occasionally blurred by trails of smoke from the engine—a charcoal drawing carelessly smudged. The very ordinary character of the winter landscape seemed at odds with the subject of my journey. I would hardly have been surprised to see an Oriental scene: towers, minarets, gilded domes glittering in a sun far more bright than that of our New England skies.

The derailment of a freight train on the track ahead, causing a delay of some four hours, shook my precarious confidence and threatened to overwhelm me with despair. I felt that the incident was foreordained—Fate's judgment on a fool's errand. Nevertheless, Fate or no, I shall write a curt note to the railroad's directors—some of whom are my acquaintances—to let them know of the enormous inconvenience to which I was subjected.

We arrived at last at four o'clock—too late to accomplish anything. I was faced then with a decision: return at once to Boston, or find—if I could—a decent hotel and begin my assault in the morning. If I returned, I feared that I might never come back. Quite aside from the mishap, the journey had been disagreeable in the extreme. Further, I feared that I might never again get up my courage to confront her. Go away, I thought, and I will never see this place again. I will never have them.

Stay, on the other hand—stay and seek her out— I weakened. I surrendered myself once again to that obsession which had held me tight in its grip since the moment I had heard of the existence of those fragments of the poet's heart. I rose from my seat, brushed the soot from my coat, and stepped out into the bitter cold, the dripping mist of the waning afternoon.

The station was crowded with people either waiting for a train or hurrying onto the one which I had just left. Here and there a bright eye, a rosy cheek, gave evidence of a human being as yet unsoiled by existence in this Temple of Industry. But most had a dull, dead look, like so many automatons. It is not surprising. What can life be chained to a machine ten hours a day?

I sought out a railway guard and asked directions to a hotel. He recommended the Merrimack House as being conveniently situated and not too dear—obviously he thought that I was a commercial traveler—but the reek of his breath was so unpleasant that I forbore to ask for an alternative. I made my way to the street, hurrying away from the blasting engines, the acrid stench that gave the depot the aspect of being a vestibule, as it were, to a cacophonous Hell.

A decrepit hack eventually conveyed me to the hotel. I saw at once what type of establishment it was, but I consoled myself with the thought that I need stay for one night only. The lobby was half-filled with sharp-looking young men—younger than I, many of them—wearing checked coats and paper collars. The poisonous vapor of their cheap cigars polluted the air; their rasping voices called back and forth in tones of oafish good fellowship. They saw that I was not one of them (I wore decent dark gray), and so, although they stared at me boldly enough, no one of them spoke to me or even nodded.

The desk clerk, after some deliberation, decided that he had a room for me after all, but when he informed me of its price I balked. Four dollars!

Warily he looked me up and down; he had little in his experience, I was sure, to prepare him to deal with an individual outside the normal run of itinerant salesmen, cotton agents, mill overseers, lecture tourers and the like.

I hesitated. I thought again of the prize which would be mine. Then all this sordid, tiresome haggling would be forgotten; then I would erase from my memory this hotel and its vulgar inhabitants and its thieving desk clerk. I paid.

A sullen boy showed me upstairs to a cubbyhole which surely must have given a bad night to anyone who feared confinement in a small space. Bed, bureau, washstand crowded together with barely room to stand between. My spirits, which had momentarily risen, sank again. But there was no turning back. I would be a fool indeed, having come so far, to abandon the search now. And so, no sooner had I seen my room (my cell, rather) than I left it and went out to the nearby shops to purchase a nightshirt and a spare collar.

I returned, deposited them in the bureau, and descended once again to get my dinner. The hotel dining room was crowded and noisy. A laden waiter motioned me to a seat at a table already occupied by a man halfway through his meal. I hesitated; I wanted no company. I wanted to spend a solitary evening plotting once again the details of my campaign. But after a moment I acquiesced. As much as I wanted solitude, I wanted my dinner more. New customers had crowded in behind me and I thought that it would be a long time before I would be able to secure a table for myself. I sat down; a waiter flying past flung a menu at me.

My companion looked up briefly from his plate, nodded, and returned to his meal as I looked at the printed card. The selection was limited: beef, mutton, or turkey, with oysters to begin. The waiter, passing again, demanded to know what I would have. I glanced at my companion's plate, the contents of which, now depleted, were undeterminable. I ordered oysters and mutton.

14

The man opposite nodded again, swallowed a large mouthful, and told me his name, which I forgot the moment he spoke it. I gave him in return *a* name—not my own—and we commenced a lopsided conversation.

He told me that he was from Albany, New York; that he was a subscription salesman for a well-known publishing house; that selling was a profitable trade for both author and seller alike if both of them trusted the seller; that he had been at his present occupation for seven years, previously having been a bank clerk. He was married, he said, and he saw his wife regularly enough to satisfy them both (this with a large wink); he had three children, he said, and produced a family photograph to prove it; he frequently came to Lowell, he said, and he could fix me up with a likely female if I was inclined to join him after supper.

To all of this I made replies so noncommittal as to be almost rude. I certainly had no intention of telling him my business in the city, and I dislike inventing convenient lies which often turn out to be inconvenient.

My meal arrived, more dead than alive, and what with much attention to the business of eating it and a well-aimed riposte now and then to my companion's discourse, I managed well enough to get through the succeeding half hour. He waited with me until I had finished, apparently still hoping that I would join him for the evening, but as we rose to leave I pleaded fatigue. I watched him go out through the lobby and then I went upstairs to my room. The food, thoroughly mediocre as it was, had revived me. I wanted to be alone with my thoughts, my hopes, my dreams of my triumph which now once again seemed so painfully close.

Who lives who does not want to touch genius? Who lives, sentient, who does not want to hear if only for a moment the music of the dreamer's sweet song? All of us, ordinary

15

mortals, know that in our midst from time to time live beings who are as different from our poor clay as diamonds from coal, as porcelain from mud, as the stars in their courses from fragments of shattered glass in the street. They commune with the angels, these special ones; and from time to time they transmit to us an echo of these intelligences. For this we are in their debt. What would be our lives without these occasional illuminations, these glimpses of a world above our own (I do not speak of Heaven), these moments when we are allowed to try to understand what it means to be genius? Genius!

Surely the world never saw such a one as him. Not that the world cared. The world ignored him, the world left him and his loved ones to starve, the world—to its everlasting shame—refused to see that for a few brief years it had in its midst a bright star—a comet flaring across the dark sky of our ignorance—and so left him to die, tragically, alone, reviled, unmourned save by a devoted few.

I trembled, thinking of it, for the thousandth, the ten thousandth time. To have seen him! To have known him, spoken to him, held his hand in friendship—to have been bathed in the fire of those brilliant eyes reflecting the phantasies, the dancing arabesques, the dark seething visions of his special netherworld of the spirit!

He had been dead ten years when I was born. I remember still the day I discovered him. It was a dreary autumn afternoon, a Saturday, and so normally a day for me to run the Common with my friends; but I had been ill with a stubborn wheezing cough, and my mother decided that I must stay at home. I wandered through the house, looking for something to amuse me—I was an only child—and eventually I found myself in my father's library, a large dim room at the rear of the house, deserted at that hour because my father, whose exclusive place it was, was downtown at his office as he was six days out of every seven.

16

I browsed the shelves of heavy, leather-bound volumes. I saw nothing that attracted my listless eye. I turned away—how I tremble to think of it! Had I not turned back for one final perusal, I might have missed what has become the very reason for my life.

I saw a small volume wedged between two larger ones. I pulled it out. The brown cover was worn, the lettering faded. Some instinct moved me to open it to the title page: *Tales of the Grotesque and Arabesque.* I had never seen such a title. It thrilled me. I sounded the syllables over and over in my mind. Helpless to remove my eyes from the table of contents, I stumbled to a plush chair by the window and sat down. I began to read.

I paused, now, in my reminiscence, reliving once again the shock of that discovery almost twenty-five years before. Never had I read anything like it; never, excepting his own work, have I read anything like it since. I heard heavy feet clumping down the hotel corridor. Someone laughed; someone—a woman—swore. I shivered, although the room was not cold. I was alone in a strange city. I had embarked upon a quest whose difficulty I could only imagine. I was traveling alien ground; only the urgency of my need—and, I admit, the growing excitement of the chase—drove me on.

Mrs. Loring, my informant, had told me enough to arouse my imagination but not nearly enough to satisfy my curiosity. They existed, she said. That was all she knew. And—imagine it!—their recipient existed also. Mrs. Loring had had it on the best authority. (What this was she did not say, and I did not inquire, attempting as I was to keep our conversation casual—and yet not so casual that I missed some vital point.)

I may add that Mrs. Loring, despite her high position in Boston society—or perhaps because of it—is not well-read. I doubt that she peruses more than a few monthly magazines and an occasional Christmas annual. I was sure that she had never read the Ingram collection published some years ago. And if that published correspondence was so deeply moving, so agonizing, so revealing of the heart of the man, what must the unpublished be? For there were unpublished items—of that Mrs. Loring was positive. Unpublished—perhaps unpublishable.

I had listened to her that evening with mounting excitement, although I had been careful not to show it. She never knew that I had more than passing interest in her gossip. She does not know, now, that I have embarked upon my search. I look forward to surprising her with an account of my adventure the next time I see her. Perhaps I will even show her a page or two.

Unpublished! A vast treasure—waiting for me! I imagined them: a thick packet, carefully wrapped and tied, brittle, discolored, the edges charred, perhaps (so high did my fancy soar), by the flames of his passion. How I longed to see them—hold them—possess them!

I switched off the electric lamp and climbed into bed. My new nightshirt scratched around my neck. I closed my eyes. His face floated up. I felt very close to him now, here, in this hotel, in this dreary city. He had been here, had seen this hotel perhaps; had passed along these thoroughfares. The population had been very different then, of course, since the heavy onslaught of European immigration had not yet begun. Perhaps the faces he saw had been brighter, prettier, more filled with the joy of life. I hoped so, for his sake.

Certainly he had found some happiness here, at the end of his brief, tortured existence. He had found one face which came, in the little time left to him, to mean more than any other. He had found peace; sanctuary; a tranquil

18

time before the final storm. He had found a love: Annie Richmond. I hoped—I prayed—to find her, too. Tomorrow.

A shudder—a wracking thrill—convulsed my body. I turned over and went to sleep.

2

IN THE MORNING, after a visit to the hotel barber and a satisfying breakfast—alone—I composed a note:

January 21

My Dear Mrs. Richmond:

It has come to my attention that some years ago you recognized the early promise of Henry Claypool Hough and that you were instrumental in securing for him the means to study in Europe.

I am at present engaged in writing a monograph on Hough's career which I plan to present to my fellow members of the Boston Art Club. I am in Lowell for a day or two. Would it be possible for me to call on you this afternoon at two o'clock? To have some details of his early life from one who recognized and encouraged his talent from the beginning would be, I assure you, a sincere honor and privilege. I promise you that I will be brief.

Believe me to be, madam, your servant—

I read the note over before I signed it and sealed the envelope. Although I had needed to use the hotel stationery, it made a satisfactory impression—the paper was thick, of fair quality, and it showed off my somewhat florid Spencerian script to good advantage. It would, I thought, do nicely.

The request for information about Henry Hough, although a subterfuge, was a perfectly reasonable one. He himself, before he died last year, paid public tribute to those who had helped him in his all too brief career, and he named Mrs. Richmond among them. She had her own talent, it seemed, for attaching herself to men of genius. And although I foresaw difficulty in getting from her what I truly sought, I could think of no reason aside from pure selfishness why she should not speak to me of Hough, who had been so much younger than she and with whom— surely!—she had had no romantic attachment. And if I could get her to speak freely of him, then perhaps, with luck, I could introduce the other and so begin to lay my siege.

With the help of the desk clerk I found a boy to take the note. I instructed him to wait for a reply. Upon inquiry, I discovered that the address on the envelope was about two miles away "up in Belvidere," wherever that was. Surely, I thought, the entire city could not be made up of the rabbit-warren tenements and monolithic factories which had formed my impression of it until now. Although I knew nothing about Mrs. Richmond (nothing, that is, except the only important thing), I was sure that the beloved "Annie" lived in a more suitable habitation than what I had seen so far.

The hotel lobby was deserted, but even had it been as heavily populated as the night before I would not have lingered. I had no more desire for companionship now than I had had then. I decided to put my time to good use and walk the streets a while, and get the feel of the place. I went out.

The day was brilliant, the sun blinding in the winter-blue sky. The hotel faced on a small triangular plaza, where rose, from a minuscule patch of snowy ground, two monuments—a bronze statue and a granite obelisk. I waited my chance to examine them more closely and got at last across the street, narrowly avoiding execution at the feet of a team of dray horses.

The statue, a winged victory, was an object of great beauty but little information. After a moment, therefore, I moved on to the other, larger memorial, upon whose massive plinth was carved the episode of the Baltimore massacre in '61. Three martyrs of that conflict—the first dead of the war—lay buried beneath the memorial stone.

Faint memory stirred. These men had been led, if I recalled my history correctly, by the infamous Butler, who later, as Governor, had unearthed the ghoulish traffic in corpses at the Tewksbury Almshouse.

A bitter wind buffeted me. I looked about to see where I should walk next. On the second side of the plaza rose an impressive pile of granite topped by a clock tower, undoubtedly City Hall. On the third side was a large square brick building of unidentifiable function; beyond it stretched a continuous row of brick houses which terminated at the far end in a mass of mill buildings. In the direction opposite the City Hall lay what appeared to be the central business district. Again at my peril I crossed the busy street and made my way towards the shops which I had passed and briefly entered the evening before.

It had long been a whim of mine to stop at bookstores

wherever I traveled and check their stock for copies of the poems or tales. As I walked now down Merrimack Street, away from the Merrimack House, not two blocks away from the Merrimack River—ah, the originality of these manufacturers in bestowing names!—I passed a stationer's whose window displayed a few cheap novels. As much to warm myself as to satisfy my curiosity, I stepped inside.

The clerk, a young man, inquired whether he could help me. I made my request; I spoke the name whose very sound sends a small shiver of excitement through my heart.

He shook his head. "Who?"

I repeated the name, laying a heavy stress upon the last short syllable.

"Don't think so—what's his latest?"

" 'The Bells,' " I said. Fool! "Eighteen forty-nine."

He glanced at me quickly to see whether I joked; when he saw that I did not, he shrugged and shook his head again. "Better try Prince's down the street. We only carry the new things."

As I left I wondered why I had been so annoyed. I had often been disappointed in such an experiment. Why had I expected to find, say, a full edition in the first stationer's I chanced upon here? Was it because this was a place—a city—he had visited? If so, then every bookseller in Boston and Providence and New York, Philadelphia and Baltimore and Richmond, should have his work in stock, and yet I knew perfectly well that they did not. He was still in print, yes, and someone—I did not know who—was collecting the royalties, but he was hardly Lew Wallace, whose *Ben-Hur,* published some years ago, was still to be had in multiple editions everywhere.

Opposite the stationer's, set well back from the street,

stood a small stone church. On one side of it a canal flowed down to the mill beyond; on the other, attached to the church, stood a square stone rectory. I paused, despite the cold, to consider the incongruity of such a building on this drab commercial thoroughfare. With its pointed, leaded windows and its squat belfry, it was extremely picturesque; it might, in a different setting, have served as a backdrop for one of his tales. It lacked only a churchyard crammed with mossy, tilted gravestones to make it complete. Here, set chockablock in the midst of a factory town, it seemed an anachronism—as he must have seemed himself.

My thoughts were interrupted by a touch on my sleeve. I looked around, annoyed, to find the source of this impertinence. My eyes fell on a child, a ragged girl, not more than ten years old. Her head was covered by a threadbare gray shawl which she held under her chin; her face was exceedingly dirty; her mouth was disfigured by a wet red sore running across the upper lip. Involuntarily I stepped back, almost colliding with a large elderly gentleman; I apologized to him and turned away. The child followed me; she touched my sleeve again. I shook her off and walked more quickly, but she trotted beside me. I felt horribly embarrassed. I stopped again.

"Get away!"

Wordlessly she stared up at my face; I was conscious that passers-by stared, too, but no one stopped to help me.

"I don't give anything. Now get away!"

For the third time she touched my sleeve; still she did not speak. It did not occur to me then that she might have been a mute; I thought that she was a foreigner who knew no English. She looked foreign, quite aside from the usual dirt which foreigners wear like armor. Her eyes were dark, her skin olive, her nose already prominent despite her youth, her forehead low and flat, her cheekbones high. God knew where she came from, but I heartily wished that she would go back.

Suddenly I felt my irritation rise like vomit in my throat. The train's delay, the sordid hotel, the ignorant bookseller—and, worst of all, the uncertainty of my success—all these flashed through my mind. This persistent supplicant was the final, unbearable aggravation. Savagely I struck at her arm. The blow threw her off balance. I did not wait to see whether she fell. Rapidly I walked away towards the further concentration of shops, towards the bookstore which had been recommended to me.

There I found a larger selection of publications, but not what I sought. I was somewhat mollified, however, by the pleasant manners of the middle-aged clerk, who was familiar with the name I spoke and who seemed sincerely sorry that he had no copies on hand. When I left the store it was almost noon. I returned along Merrimack Street to the hotel, seeing no sign of the beggar child, and inquired at the desk for a message. There was none—the boy had returned without a reply.

Odd! I had expected some word, after all—at best an invitation; at worst a brusque refusal. Silence—nothing—unsettled me for a moment and cast me back again into that agonizing doubt from which I had suffered the previous day. No reply—not even to an inquiry about Hough! Was she ill, perhaps? Dying?

I paid the boy and went to have my lunch. I had made up my mind: As soon as I had done eating, I would go myself to see her.

3

"Is Mrs. Richmond at home?"

The woman who peered at me from the narrowly opened door waited for a moment—a telling moment—before she replied, thus revealing that an answer in the negative would be a lie.

She was, from what I could see of her, middle-aged, apron-swathed, gray-haired, narrow-faced, suspicious of a stranger as they always are who serve a recluse.

Finally, as if it were a great effort, she said, "Who is calling?"

I gave her my name and my card. I thought it unlikely that my note would have been read by, or discussed with, the housekeeper; therefore I anticipated no reaction, adverse or otherwise, to my identification. In this I was correct. Her expression stayed stolidly the same as she considered, alternately, me and my pasteboard rectangle. I did not care how long she hesitated. I feared only that she would shut me out altogether, leaving me to pull the bell and pound the door and make a general nuisance of myself, which, most emphatically, I did not want to do. In a matter so delicate I felt that it was important that at all costs I maintain my dignity—although not, of course, at the cost of my ultimate success.

At last she said, "I'll see. What's your business?"

I was alert for this trap; the eager importunations which would have betrayed a less self-controlled man did not find their way past my lips.

"I am inquiring on behalf of the Boston Art Club whether she would accept an award from us. It is a great honor for her, I assure you."

Here I ventured a smile. Few women, solitary, subservient, can resist a placating grimace from a gentleman who casts himself, so to speak, upon their merciful bosoms. She did not smile in return—naturally not—but I saw in her dull eye a glimmer—the faintest spark—of response to my plea, and I knew that my first assault—to open the closed door—had been won.

I was taken aback, therefore, when with a sharp command—"Wait!"—she slammed shut the door and, presumably, went to inquire what should be done with me.

Angry epithets swarmed to my tongue. I banished them. She was, after all, simply doing her job as she saw it. I had anticipated difficulties before I began this quest; now, encountering them, I needed to be clever and resourceful and above all calm. I would win in the end; and meanwhile I must maintain control over both myself and others.

I heard no sound from within the house—although what sound I might have expected I could not say. In my mind's eye I went with my interrogator, to an upstairs sitting room perhaps, and tried to see the face of her mis-

28

tress, hear the voice, gaze upon those eyes that had gazed on *him*—

No. I could not allow myself to wander so. I would become distraught, the excitement was too great. Everything would come in time; I needed only to progress, step by careful step, slowly, tactfully, ever mindful of the ultimate goal.

To calm myself I paced back and forth on the wide porch, or verandah, which surrounded the house. This was indeed a different place from the congested red brick and decaying wood of the central city. Mrs. Richmond's home was situated on the Andover Road, which, parallel to the river below, led up a hill overlooking the smoke-spewing factories. As I reached the corner of the verandah I saw that a small garden, now buried in snow, extended behind the house to the mound of a low wall or hedge; then the ground dropped precipitously away to the river. Through bare trees I could see the hills of the opposite shore. It was a picturesque spot. Had she lived here, I wondered, when she knew him?

The house itself was an example of that decaying splendor which so enchanted the romantic mind of the architect of Usher. After a moment's consideration of its style I decided that it had most probably been built after the middle of the century, and would not therefore have been a place which he had visited. It was an ornate and sizable structure, originally gray but now bearing large, unsightly splotches where the paint had peeled, exposing the bare wood underneath. Its design followed no particular pattern, thus classing it with what has become known as the Gothic style—a turret here, a balcony there, windows at every unexpected level; the whole—quite large—giving an effect of wealth departed, proud display fallen on hard times. I had noticed as I approached that several shutters hung at odd angles; the shrubbery grew untamed so high around the first-floor windows that the interior rooms must have been in shadow even on so bright a day as this.

The house stood some distance from the road. I stepped down off the porch and walked a few paces back along the graveled drive to get a better look at the fortress to which I had lain siege; even so, I was hardly within calling distance of the hack driver who waited just beyond the gate. I turned to look at the facade rising before me. I allowed my imagination a moment's play. I might, I thought, have been a character in one of the tales, preparing to enter that forbidding portal, where I would find—what? The toothsome Berenice? The phantasm Ligeia?

I shook my head. Stay awake! I was conscious just then of a movement at one of the second-floor windows. For an instant—a fraction of a second only—I saw a face. It was a woman's face, I thought, but so swift had been its appearance that I could have identified it no further.

I smiled to myself. It was just the thing, that face—the perfect touch. A house such as this was incomplete without the appearance, briefly, at an upper window, of one of its inhabitants—an inhabitant who might, in such a place, be only a spirit, a ghost of happier times, seeking that soul to whom long years ago she had pledged her own. Ah, and where was *it*?

The door opened. I ran back to the porch; I bounded loudly up the warping steps. Without a word the housekeeper—surely she was the housekeeper!—stood back to let me in. After closing the door she directed me across the wide entrance hall to the front parlor. She did not offer to take my hat and coat. I passed in, murmuring my thanks; I felt a little shock in the region of my heart when I realized that she had shut that door, too, firmly behind me.

30

The room was dim—of course!—and for a moment I was at a disadvantage, forced to wait until my eyes had adjusted to the gloom before I could see who—what?—awaited me.

I discerned a woman's figure near the shaded window. I bowed at it. "Madam."

"I am not 'Madam.'"

"I beg your pardon. I had asked to see—"

"My mother. She is not at home."

She made no move to come to me, and so, awkwardly holding my hat, I took a few tentative steps toward her. I was better able to see now, and what presented itself to my vision was neither more nor less than I had expected: a large room, whose elaborate furnishings in the heavy mock-Renaissance style of twenty years previous were crowded together, all carved and brocaded, tufted velvet on buhl, in a frantic attempt (so it seemed) to prove the owner's station in life by the quantity of his display. Dark red draperies hung from gilded poles at the windows; the darkly patterned walls were covered with thick-framed landscapes and fading mezzotints; a worn Turkey carpet covered the floor. Every available surface—tabletops, mantel, what-nots—was obliterated by china figurines, morsels of carved bone, artificial flowers under glass, all evidence of ample money to spend on such bric-a-brac. And yet every object, every piece of furniture, every lamp and figurine seemed out of place, secondhand, as if it were displayed in a not very well patronized antiquarian's shop. This was a room which had been decorated—mercilessly—a generation or more ago. Nothing had been changed since that initial effort.

The woman who received me was another matter. She, too, looked out of date, worn, slightly déclassé. But her voice was strong and clear, and her face, which must once have been pretty, was still firm and clean-featured. Her brow was high, her nose well-shaped, her chin rather alarmingly long. She was, I judged, about forty years of age—a few years older than I—and if she had taken any trouble about her appearance, she might have passed for thirty. She wore a stained brown smock over a drab skirt; as far as I could tell no corset trimmed her rather full figure; her light brown hair was pulled into a careless knot; and her handsome mouth—a feature by which many women make their fortune—had that peculiar strained look common to females who have given up whatever struggle it is that women must make.

"Then I am doubly sorry to trouble you. I wrote a note this morning asking Mrs. Richmond for a brief interview—"

"Yes. I saw it."

"May I ask if she did also?"

"She did."

"Ah, yes—well." I cleared my throat in feigned confusion. For purposes of achieving one's objective, it is safe to classify together both the solitary housekeeper and the solitary daughter of the recluse, the difference being that with the daughter one may be sure of a slightly less suspicious reception. I smiled at her.

"You do understand that I will not impose—"

"You are imposing now."

"With only the most unselfish of motives, I assure you. I ask nothing for myself. I want only to present him—Hough—as best I can, and since he himself so specifically mentioned Mrs. Richmond—"

"She can tell you nothing."

"But she knew him—he was born here; he was a neighbor, was he not? She saw his first work—"

"She can tell you nothing. And she would not if she could."

"May I ask why? I do not mean to press, but I have come a fair distance, and if I am to fail, then at least perhaps you can give me a reason."

She shook her head slowly. As she did so a pale shaft of light just caught her eyes and I saw that they were gray—like "Annie's" eyes; like the eyes of the woman in "Landor's Cottage." I felt a little thrill.

"He does not deserve to be—monographed." The clear, firm voice held now a bitter note which puzzled me.

"He has a very fair reputation. One of his portraits was recently hung in the museum in Copley Square."

"He is dead only a year. In another decade he will be forgotten." Harsher and more harsh—why?

"Even so—we cannot tell, can we, what will happen to his name? Perhaps you are right, perhaps not. But for now—just in case you are mistaken—do you not think that we owe it to posterity to record all we can about him from those who knew him best?"

"You cannot be serious." She was clearly angry now.

"I assure you that I am."

"You want my mother to talk to you about him?" Her hand had found the back of a carved rosewood chair; she gripped it, hard, so that I saw the straining tendons. What emotion had produced that painful clasp? It was her left hand. I saw no ring.

"Yes—if she will be so kind."

"Henry Hough? Born in Lowell in eighteen fifty? Studied here and in Boston until eighteen seventy-two? Then went, with the help of friends—my mother among them—to Paris to study?"

"Yes."

"Traveled to Munich in eighteen eighty-one?"

"Yes."

"Exhibited there at the Royal Academy?"

"Yes."

"Then went to Florence, where he died?"

"Yes."

She paused, then, in her interrogation, whether to study me further or to find the words to order me out of the house I could not tell. I was by this time thoroughly confused. What had gone wrong? Why was she so hostile? This was no refusal of an interview; this was a cross-examination about a man who had been her mother's protégé and who by all accounts—her own opinion notwithstanding—had in every way justified her mother's prescient encouragement of his talent.

Suddenly, from the floor above, we heard a peremptory thump—three sharp, echoing raps. Both of us looked involuntarily to the ceiling; her eyes lingered there after mine had returned to her face. When finally she lowered her gaze again, her anger seemed to have vanished. In its place was an expression even more alarming, for it took the game, which until now I had been struggling to play, completely out of my hands and informed me unquestionably that she had won.

"Now," she said coldly, "why don't you tell me really why you came?"

4

"No—" SHE put out her hand as if to ward me off. "Don't tell me. Let me guess. You came—in search of some-thing—of some*one*—far greater than Henry Hough."

My silence was my assent.

"There have been others before you."

I nodded.

"Some of them had very good credentials. They were from universities: they offered secure and permanent sanctuary. Glass cases, locks, dignified display—"

I simply stared at her, hoplessly outflanked.

"Why should she give to you the items which they sought—or even talk to you about them—if she would not give them up to all those others?"

I fumbled for some reply. It seemed important to me now that I at least make her understand why I had tried. Finally a few words came.

"'Secure and permanent sanctuary'—to be pawed by generations of ignorant students? She was right to keep them. She could not want that—his most private feelings, so eloquently expressed to her, on display for all the world to see. No—" Ah, what could I say? I was not even speaking to the right person, which was fortunate, perhaps, since I was so sadly lacking in eloquence. "She must give them to someone who cherishes his memory as she does. She must give them to someone who cares—very much, more than life itself—for his name. And hers, of course."

Weak, weak—my stomach cramped as I watched contempt suffuse her face. She had no right—

"Why not give them to me, then?" she said. "What makes you think that she will let them get away at all? I am the logical person, am I not, to receive such a treasure?"

This was true—unarguably true—but since I had not known of her existence until twenty minutes before, I had no answer. Blast Mrs. Loring, whose information, so tantalizingly sparse, now proved to be fatally so!

I looked again at the ceiling from whence had come those peremptory—those provocative thumps. *She* was there, above us, not a moment away—and yet she might have been with him in the grave, for all I should see of her. I had planned, in my innocence, to make my case in person, slowly, artfully, gently leading her on, gaining her trust, so that when the crucial moment came, and at last I asked her for her treasure, she would not be startled or frightened but would respond to me as a confidant, someone who shared with her a mutual devotion to his bright memory.

Now my plan had been wrecked; I was beaten even before I began. My assault—my siege—had been deflected as easily as a stout shield deflects a wooden sword. I should have to leave without ever seeing "Annie." I was seized with a sudden urge to bolt, to run up the stairs, burst through the door of her room, throw myself at her feet, beg, plead, *force* her to hear me.

Of course I did nothing of the sort. I swallowed, painfully, and extended my hand to my companion. She ignored it; she looked steadily at me while I stood with my arm outstretched, frozen like the victim of the bad fairy's curse. What did I see in her eyes? In her face? She was hostile no longer, now that she had vanquished me; no—not hostile, not angry at the impertinence (for so she surely thought of it) of my request. Rather, her expression, implacable as it was, seemed to have softened. If I read her right—and I was sure I did—she seemed now to look at me with unmistakable pity. Pity! From such a woman! Surely she had no packet of letters, no treasure to console the long empty years of her life! No genius had ever loved her, immortalized her in a single perfect poem. What right had she, then, to pity anyone?

Abruptly I broke the spell, withdrew my hand. With the briefest of bows I turned and left the room. I left the house, I hurried out into the afternoon and trotted down the drive to my hack. I flung myself onto the cracked leather seat and ordered the driver away. I wanted only to get quit of that house, to unburden myself of that unbearable sense of defeat which weighted down my heart.

I closed my eyes and abandoned myself to the rattling progress of the carriage. Pity! From a solitary maiden lady! (Of course I did not know that she was never married. She might have been a widow. I simply assumed it. When subsequent events proved me correct, I was able at least to have the small consolation of one right guess in the morass of my mistakes.)

I felt a tear slide down my cheek, and then another. I sat back in my small space and abandoned myself to my grief.

I would as soon have stayed in that smelly, jolting box forever; I did not want to arrive anywhere. Before me lay the hotel, the business of paying the bill for my meals, getting to the depot, again enduring the railway carriage for another tiresome, bone-wrenching journey, arriving—empty-handed—at Back Bay to re-enter a life from which all hope, all light, had vanished now that I had not gotten my prize.

We stopped. I opened my eyes and looked through the dirty glass. We were caught in traffic; we were stranded in a sea of conveyances on what seemed to be a main thoroughfare. Here, in the smoke-clogged center of the city, the fading day had dimmed to dusk, although it was hardly past four o'clock. Lights had come on in the shops; in front of windows filled with merchandise I saw the silhouetted figures of passers-by. Most of them hurried past, spurred on by the cold, but a few lingered at the displays and occasionally someone went in or out.

Happy populace! Not one of them suffered a burden such as mine. Not one of them thought beyond the week's rent, the grocer's bill, an evening of cards to break the placid routine of their lives. Not one of them suffered that hunger for the unattainable which, unassuaged, gnaws ever deeper, ever deadlier at the soul.

We lurched ahead. I was tired; I was very cold. The effort of alighting, tending to my affairs at the hotel, getting myself away, seemed beyond me. Every clop-clop of the horse's hooves took me farther away from her, farther away from what had been until today my short sweet dream of triumph. I thought of her there, sitting in her room, summoning her daughter, demanding an explanation of the caller's business. What would she think? Perhaps she would think nothing, perhaps her daughter would say that I was a salesman of some sort. Or perhaps she would go on with the fraudulent note— No. Hough's name had evoked a painful memory, more painful even than the real object of my call. Would she, then, tell Mrs. Richmond the truth—that I had come for the ultimate prize, the invaluable tokens of her connection with *him?*

And how, I wondered, would Mrs. Richmond receive that news? How had she received it before? Did she even know of those previous attempts? Or did the daughter intercept all callers, all supplicants? Did she guard the mother with so strict a vigilance because she wanted to protect her from the importunations of eager devotees, or because she wanted to keep the treasure for herself? How had Ingram acquired his few specimens?

An unpleasant thought occurred to me; it startled me so that I sat up straight and almost fell to the dirty floor of the carriage as we turned a corner.

What if Mrs. Richmond was, after all, quite willing to part with them?

What if she would be glad to give them—or sell them— to someone who would care for them with a devotion equal to her own?

What if she never knew that anyone wanted them?

What if—my heart beat painfully in my agitated breast—what if her rapping, her tapping, the peremptory thumps (of her cane?) had been a signal—not to the daughter, but to me? Had she been attempting to call for help? There were surely not many visitors to that house, which stood at some distance from its neighbors on the sparsely populated road; it would be not at all difficult to isolate an old woman (in failing health?) from those who would rescue her, not only for her own sake but for the sake of that one who had loved her, unwisely perhaps but devotedly all the same—

We stopped again. I looked out and saw the hotel. I

39

threw open the door and sprang out; I paid the driver—too well!—and hurried inside. What to do? What to *do*? I needed to think, to plan—ah, now I had a challenge indeed!

Late afternoon stragglers clustered in the lobby. I ignored them. I went to the saloon bar and ordered a double whiskey. I needed to calm myself; I needed to make a plot which would outwit even the crafty Dupin. The liquor burned down my throat and into my stomach; it gave me new life. O evil dragon! No knight was ever more determined than I to slay thee! No knight ever yearned more to reach the sacred prize within!

Tomorrow, I thought. Tomorrow I will begin again.

5

"Is Miss Richmond at home?"

Again the suspicious servant, again the revealing pause. But now there was no interrogation, no command to wait. She simply stared at me and then, assuming that I understood the process, shut the door on my smiling face while she went to inquire.

I did not stroll the grounds this day. The weather had turned, a fine sleet fell, the wind was raw from the east. Further, I did not want to leave the cover of the porch and expose myself to whatever eyes might peer from one of the upstairs windows. For Mrs. Richmond herself to see me—for her possibly to try to signal me—would only complicate my plan. I did not want to see her—to alert her—until the decisive moment. It was the daughter now with whom I must treat; and then, having slain the dragon (a mere figure of speech!), I would claim the victor's share.

The door opened. I walked past the guardian servant into the hall. I entered the parlor, darker than ever on this dark morning. I heard the door close behind me, as before; I looked around me, blinking, as before; and when my eyes had grown accustomed to the gloom, I saw that I was alone.

I thought it curious that I—surely an unwelcome caller—should be left by myself freely to examine their things. Did they not fear that I would slip some small memento into my pocket? Did they not suspect that I might slide open a drawer of the ebony side table and scrabble for a specimen autograph (if not his, then hers)? Despite everything I could not but think that such treatment of me—such neglect, if you will—amounted to an indirect judgment of my character. They might deny my request, but still they knew that they dealt with a gentleman. Comforting thought!

I surveyed the room. I saw nothing of interest. My impression of the day before had been correct—it was a faded, outmoded chamber which twenty years previous might have been in the height of fashion. Only the small Steinway in the corner, shawl-draped, keys covered, and the porcelain clock on the mantel gave any indication of the owners' good taste—these, and a large handsome bookcase between the front windows.

I heard the click of the latch. I turned. Miss Richmond stood in the doorway.

"You!"

I bowed; I felt the smile upon my face.

"Dear lady—I could not leave the city without seeing you again. My behavior yesterday was inexcusable—and yet I have come to ask you to excuse it all the same. I am sure you understand that it was my devotion—my adoration, if you will—which impelled me to behave with such presumption, such utter lack of good manners. In short, my dear Miss Richmond, I could not leave this city—forever!—without your forgiveness. I hope you do not find me too bold in asking *that!*"

I had rehearsed this effusion a dozen times in my cell at the Merrimack House, and always with the same result—I saw her, in my imagination, melt under the warmth of my fervor; I saw her extend her hand in absolution if not in friendship, and thus advance me to point two in my renewed attack. So sure had I been of the effect of my words upon her maidenly ears that I had not considered what I would do if once again I were rebuffed.

She stared at me. No dragon ever turned so baleful an eye; had she been able to snort flames, the room would have been a bonfire.

She raked me up and down with her glance. Finally—it seemed an hour—she spoke:

"Do not think that because we are three women alone we are without recourse. I have only to scream and Triphena will run to the neighbors'."

"Please! Do not—I mean no harm. I am going, I swear it. But I realized yesterday after I left that I had deeply distressed you, and I could not sleep all night for thinking of—of what you were thinking of me."

There is a natural human impulse, not exclusively the property of religion, to comfort the penitent. Now, at last, I saw a hint of that amiable reaction begin to soften her face.

"You are a fraud and a liar as well. Why should you care what I think?" Her voice was noticeably less hard.

"Because—because you are close to *her*." It was the wrong note; quickly I changed it. "Because you are a lady, you are sensitive and delicate; you are far too fine a person to be harassed as I have harassed you."

"Nonsense." Softer still.

"I assure you—we men have feelings, too, believe me. Our souls are as easily scarred as yours—with the difference that we must hide our grief; we cannot weep it out upon a sympathetic shoulder."

I swear that her glance traveled for an instant to that portion of my anatomy. I felt an intoxicating warmth begin to spread over my body. I watched her struggle with herself.

"No. I suppose you cannot." Her tone was almost quiet now, almost conversational.

"And—because we are so restrained—we often hold our sorrow longer than you, and it feeds on us, and debilitates us, and wounds us altogether more fatally than it does you."

Again she looked me over. "You do not look wounded to me."

"Ah, dear lady—!" I pressed my hand to my vest. "The wound is here—within—hidden! Festering!"

Suddenly she laughed—a startling sound. I had the sense to remain solemn.

"You are a fraud! Absolutely! What's the matter—are you an agent for someone? Have you a wealthy client whom you fear to disappoint?"

"No one but myself. And although I prefer your smile to your frown, I can assure you that a passion such as mine is nothing to laugh at. I am utterly sincere in everything I say."

She came toward me; she peered into my face. "Were you sincere about Henry Hough?"

I blushed; I could not help it. How much rope I had given her to hang me!

"I did not want to alarm you."

"No? And so you chose the very topic which alarms us more than any other."

"I did not know—"

"Precisely! And you did not know because you did not do your homework! If you had taken more than the most cursory look at his career, you would have known that his is the name most calculated to distress us."

I shook my head. "I am sorry. You are right, of course. It was very stupid of me."

"Yes. It was."

"But he did thank her, publicly—"

"He did, yes. Although a kinder man might have omitted her name and so spared her feelings."

"I beg your pardon. I simply do not know what you are talking about."

She looked away; she bit her lips. Go on, I thought. I feared to say anything. Let it come out, I thought, I will not divulge it—

"He did a series of etchings. Satiric cartoons. He rather fancied himself another Thomas Nast. He was wrong, of course—Nast caricatures those who deserve it, but Hough simply picked on innocent people for no reason at all. The cartoons were autobiographical—'A Merry Life,' he called them. They represented his own progress from childhood to adult. Family, friends, teachers, European associates—they were all there."

"I have never seen them—or even heard of them."

"He struck off only a dozen of each. I do not imagine that any of them are even in this country. But someone saw them—someone here, who was traveling in Germany —and of course when he returned, he told everyone about Hough's little joke. All Europe, he said, had laughed at them."

"They were—unflattering?"

"They were obscene. He reviled everyone he had ever known—everyone who had ever helped him. Even his mistresses—yes, he kept two or three women, one of them

45

bore him a child and he even included her! The mother of his son!" Her voice trembled. "Every character he drew was completely—unclothed. And engaged in unspeakable—"

She broke off. She took a long breath. "I do not need to elaborate. You understand."

"Yes," I said. "I do. Will you forgive me?"

She turned to face me again. I put out my hand, and this time she took it. Our eyes met as I felt her flesh touch mine. It seemed that one of us should say something—some light and careless thing to ease the strain, to slide us past the awkward moment—but neither of us spoke. There are times when silence is more eloquent than any words, when conversation covers up an emotion suddenly, alarmingly bared like a woman's ankle.

Thump! Thump!

I would not have been surprised, just then, had it been my heart so loud. But, as before, it was the inhabitant from the floor above. All of a sudden—how had I lost it!—I remembered my grand design, my passionate purpose. Surely—now—I could see her?

She withdrew her hand; she lowered her eyes.

"Excuse me," she said. "I must . . . go."

"To her?"

"Yes."

"Is she an invalid?"

"No, she is in good health."

"Then why—?" But it was obvious; I did not need to ask. The unmarried daughter laying waste her life in her mother's service is a familiar type. A spasm of sympathy contracted my heart. Poor daughter!

Thump! Thump!

"Do you—could you ask her?—no, not *that*. If I could see her for a moment, simply to meet her, to look at someone *he* once loved—I will not say a word to distress her, I promise."

She hesitated. Despite the urgent sound, she had not yet turned away.

"Trust me," I said. "I will do no harm."

She gazed at me, considering me. "All right," she said at last. "No—stay here. I will bring her down."

I realized that I was trembling.

"You do not know how much this means to me."

Still she lingered. "Don't I?"

"You cannot."

"How much, then does it mean? To see her for five minutes?"

"It means—"

The door opened. She whirled around, badly startled; she uttered a small exclamation of what was surely annoyance.

Annie Richmond stood before me.

47

6

To DESCRIBE my emotions at that instant is a task beyond my powers. Shock—fear—wonder—a very dreadful Awe—overwhelmed me. I could not speak, I could not move. I simply stood and stared at her, praying that she was in fact herself and not a vision conjured up by my busy brain.

She spoke, and then—alas!—I knew that she was real.

"I called three times. Are you deaf?"

Although my companion's face was turned away from me, although the light was so dim, I saw the color rise to her neck and cheek.

"I am sorry, Mama, I was just—"

"*Who* is this?" She peered at me. "Who are you? What do you want?"

Soothing phrases surged to my lips and died away. I was still trying to take her in; I was unable simultaneously to do that and to engage in further verbal fabrication.

The daughter was quicker than I. She introduced me, and then, to my astonishment (*what* was she thinking of?) she took up my discredited plan and offered it to its victim.

"He is the man who is writing a monograph on Henry Hough, Mama. You remember. He wanted to talk to you about him."

Mrs. Richmond had not taken her eyes from my face. Now she advanced with a surprisingly firm step, despite her cane, and planted herself directly in front of me. From what her daughter had told me, I half expected her to swoon—to faint into my arms—at the mention of the ingrate's name, but she remained quite calm, she spoke evenly and without constraint.

"I had your note—was it yesterday? I sent no reply because I am frequently asked about—Hough. I rarely answer. I cannot imagine why people bother about him. He is thoroughly second-rate."

At last I was sufficiently composed to take my cue and speak my lines.

"Surely it is too soon to tell?"

"It is never too soon. Mediocrity, or talent, or genius show themselves at the very first. If one can see."

A faint smile twitched at her withered lips. I tore my eyes from them and the thoughts which they aroused and shuffled into the trappings of my part.

"Not everyone is so perspicacious. There is as yet no general—no universally accepted—opinion on his work. And, in the meantime, some of us—ah—are trying to accumulate what information we can."

"Just in case."

"Just in case, yes."

"As I said, I rarely answer written inquiries about Henry Hough. I am an old woman, I have no time to write what I

50

know." (Ah, I thought, if only you would!) "But—since you are here—"

She paused to think what tidbit of intelligence she might toss at me. I was aware of the daughter watching us—watching *me*. Was she truly a dragon? Or, in repulsing me, had she simply tried to anticipate her mother's wishes? She had regained her composure; I could read nothing in her face. But the fact that she had so briskly taken up my story—which she knew to be false—gave me courage again. I had, it seemed, an ally—at least for the moment. I did not care to inquire too closely into her motive for helping me.

Mrs. Richmond turned to her daughter. "Do you know the brown trunk in the attic?"

"Near the window?"

"There is no trunk near the window, as you would know if you ever bothered to look. It is in the corner, behind the dress forms—never mind. I will go myself. Come along and see that I don't break my neck."

"Can't Triphena?"

"Triphena has work to do—which is more than I can say for some of us. Come along."

With a final, unreadable look at me Miss Richmond turned to follow her mother. Once again I was alone, but with such thoughts for company!

I seated myself on a horsehair sofa near the fireplace and chuckled softly. I could not help it: I was, as they say, tickled pink. In ten minutes' time I had advanced my plan by an hour! And—immeasurably more important—I had deceived only one person instead of two, and still I advanced. Why? Does she trust me so much, that daughter, that she is willing to plot with me against her own mother? Or—sobering thought—has she decided to use me, somehow, in some campaign of her own? My percep-

51

tions of her had changed so swiftly that I was more than a little confused. What was her game? That she was not in fact a dragon was now obvious—the mother ruled here, the daughter obeyed. The mother needed no rescuer, no knight to storm the castle.

What, then? I could not sort it out. I did not try. I could only deal with things as they came, and in the process hold fast to my original purpose.

I had seen her! That alone was a triumph. In the flesh! And although this woman was not the "Annie" whom he gave to the world, she was a very creditable successor. He had, after all, known her almost fifty years ago.

She was in fact very beautiful—for an old woman. Her hair was purest white, her eyes clear gray, her skin fine and soft, hardly wrinkled. She was, of course, slightly bent with age, and obviously she had had some trouble walking—hence the cane. But her costume was elegant, even at this hour of the morning. She wore little diamonds in her ears, a gold brooch at her throat, lace at her neck and wrists. Her dress and shawl were of a pale, indeterminate color somewhere between purple and gray. Altogether, I thought, a *grande dame*. In my euphoria I forgave her her sharp tongue; obviously—was she not now, at this moment, seeking items to help me?—it hid a kind and sympathetic heart. I decided that I liked her very much.

My opinion of the daughter was neither so favorable nor so firm. She did not run to type so neatly as her mother—she was considerably more difficult to assess. Why, for instance, did the child of so handsome a woman dress like a factory operative? She was not at all bad-looking. Why did she not try to capitalize on her appearance in the way of most women? I could not help but feel that the image which she presented was a kind of statement—a rebuff, if you will. She refused, apparently, to cater to men's taste—undoubtedly because she had given up hope of snaring one of us for her own. I decided that for the moment, at least, I would refuse to be so put off. I would treat her as I would have treated the most beautiful, the most desirable woman in the world; I would treat her, I thought, as *he* had treated her mother. Perhaps some good would come of it—and certainly I could do no harm. She was, I thought, a perfect puzzle. Why did she become distraught—furious!—at the name of a man who had insulted her mother, while the mother herself behaved with perfect equanimity?

Patience, I thought. It will come. You will discover—yes!—everything. If Mrs. Richmond, despite her daughter's objections, is so kind as to help so quickly to display one former friendship, then almost certainly she will soon—soon!—be willing to unveil another.

I heard them descend the stairs. I stood up. Mrs. Richmond came in first, leaning rather heavily on her cane, followed by her daughter carrying a sheaf of papers.

"Put them on the table," said the mother. "And light the lamp so that we can see. I want to have a look at some of these myself . . ." (this to me) "I had forgotten I had so much."

Miss Richmond did as she was told. The three of us pulled chairs to the round, silk-shawled table and, as Mrs. Richmond glanced at each item, her daughter passed it to me without looking at it. I saw at once that this was the real thing—a vein of purest gold. I could only imagine what the full mine must contain. Letters, sketches, exhibition programs, newspaper clippings—it was all there, for anyone who cared.

I of course did not care, but I performed mightily as if I did. I took out my pocket notebook; I made assiduous entries. I think that even Miss Richmond herself half believed my exclamations of surprise and delight. Certainly her mother did. She watched, amused, as I seized upon each item.

"Look!" I exclaimed. I held up a faded letter. (If only it had been one of *his!*) "This is from Paris—August 16, 1872—he had just arrived, had he not?"

"He went in June. That was the second letter. I don't know whether I have the first."

"Dear lady! I will not criticize when you are so kind, but do you mean to say that you may have . . . ah . . . mislaid some things?"

"Yes. I may have." She shrugged; her diamonds glittered in the lamplight. She looked at me with an expression of mingled irritation and amusement (a most intriguing combination). "He was never . . . terribly important to me. I am surprised that I have this much."

I suppressed a shudder; I kept a pleasant smile upon my face. Surely—surely!—she would have been more careful with those other, those inexpressibly more valuable communications!

They watched me while I browsed. The only sounds in the room were the rustle of the papers, the staccato sleet upon the windows. I did not care—I did not dare—to meet the daughter's eye. I felt sure that she was waiting for me to trip myself up, to betray myself. Would she, I wondered, enjoy my discomfiture? Or was she secretly hoping that I would succeed—at least with Hough?

By the end of half an hour I had learned more than I ever wanted to know about Henry Claypool Hough. I learned of his professed gratitude to his patrons, including Mrs. Richmond; I learned the names, ages, occupations, and avocations of those patrons; I learned that Hough, although poor, was not so poor that he could not afford a series of model/mistresses, one of whom, Claire Bernard, produced a son; I learned that he sorely missed (so he said) the heartening encouragement of his friends in America and particularly in his native city, but that all the same he never found the opportunity to return to them; I learned— But it did not matter. I learned and forgot in the same moment. Despite the importance of this little curtain raiser, I began to tire of it. I longed to get on to the play itself.

At last I assembled the scattered papers into a neat pile and placed them in front of her. I shook my head in mock amazement.

"I don't know how to thank you. This was more than I had dreamed of finding."

She regarded me. "Was it?"

"But of course. I had hoped most of all for a few reminiscences of his youth, a few of your choicer memories, perhaps a letter or two—but this!"

"Too much?"

"Ah—no, not too much, there can never be too much, although for a monograph it is perhaps too great a wealth of detail—"

"What are the requirements for a monograph?"

"Well—an overview, an introduction merely—some sense of the man—some focus on a particular aspect of his career—"

"Perhaps you should expand it. Why not do a book?"

I laughed in a self-effacing way. "Books are major projects. I had not intended to devote my life to Henry Hough."

She smiled at me. I saw what that smile must once have been. My heart turned over. "And yet you still do not have sufficient material, if what you say is correct." She paused for an excruciating moment; then, very soft, "I have not yet begun to reminisce."

7

NATURALLY I stayed to lunch. The faithful Triphena, informed of my presence, cast a swift and reproachful look at me and then retreated to her little domain to cope as best she could. Excellently, as it turned out: I had never had a better fish chowder, and her biscuits were puffs of heavenly cloud.

During the meal we spoke of everyday things. I told them a little about myself, and they in turn told me the same. Mr. Richmond, it seemed, had died some years before; he had owned a small cotton mill—nothing grand, but enough to support his wife and daughter very well and leave them a generous legacy. (They did not say this last explicitly. I am interpolating.) Mrs. Richmond touched lightly on Hough as she talked of the city's well-known native sons; and as she discoursed for a time with provincial pride on its history and its growth, I saw a curious expression in her daughter's eyes. Not hostility—nothing so definite—but rather almost sorrow, as if the old woman spoke upon a topic for which she had not adequately prepared. Particularly when Mrs. Richmond spoke of the large population of mill operatives—the immigrant class—I saw her daughter's face harden, and close, and I wondered why a maiden lady of good family, with sufficient income, should object, as she so obviously did, to criticism of those unwashed hordes which threaten to overwhelm our native American people. Mrs. Richmond did not dwell on the subject, however, and soon her daughter's expression cleared. I was happy to see it. I wanted no filial argument to divert us.

Really, Mrs. Richmond was most charming. Her initial bad temper had been, I thought, an aberration. Her voice was light and sweet, her manner gentle (with just enough vinegar, so to speak, to give it flavor). Her gray eyes, deepset, luminous, reflected that spiritual elevation, that purity of heart, which had so enchanted *him*; and as I sat at her side, and listened, and looked, I could not help but feel the sense of peace—the refuge found at last—which he must have felt when, to his joy, he found her.

The daughter spoke very little. She sat across from me, separated from me by an expanse of polished mahogany, silver, crystal, and watched her mother speak, and watched my reaction, and kept her thoughts very much to herself. I wondered if she now regretted her introduction of me to her mother. She could perfectly well (as we both knew) have passed me off as a salesman, or as a solicitor for some charity, or as any one of a dozen other types. But she had chosen (how impulsively?) to take me at my word, although she knew that word was false. Was she sorry, now, for having done so?

I warned myself not to analyze too deep. The situation

was really very simple: Two bored and lonely women had received a charming (I hoped!) and sympathetic caller; like the sensible creatures they were, they were getting the maximum enjoyment from his visit. Certainly Mrs. Richmond seemed happy to have a new audience. The more she talked the more she had to say; I could only guess at the isolation of her life, the long years of keeping her chatter to herself because everyone she knew had heard it all before. Go on, I thought, go on and on. Accustom yourself to telling me everything, so that when we come to *him*—as we will, as we will—you can simply continue comfortably as before and not feel suddenly indiscreet.

We lingered over our coffee; they professed delight at my cigar. There was a small pause while I lit it. I felt the daughter's eyes steady upon me. I glanced up, puffing; through clouds of smoke I smiled at her. The room was draughty; a sudden current blew the smoke back into my face; I coughed and wept, and so did not see whether she smiled in return.

At last we left the table. Mrs. Richmond led us into the hall; she gestured to a place on the wall by the first landing of the staircase.

"I must not forget the purpose of your visit," she said graciously. "Up there—you see the large portrait—is my only major example of Henry's work." She led the way up the stairs. "Indeed, I do not know if it could be called 'major,' since he painted it before he went away, before he had his European training. But I have always liked it. It is, I think, a good example of his flair for capturing faces. A second-rate flair, of course."

We reached the landing; I ascended a few steps beyond the turn so as to get a better view. They stood below me, just by the portrait.

It is always a curious thing to see a painting and its subject side by side yet separated by a span of years. The woman—the flesh and blood woman—whom I saw was an attractive, charming example of the sex in the autumn—the winter—of life. No one, seeing her, knowing nothing of her history, would have guessed that she was anything but what she seemed to be—a proper New England lady, a sterling example of that Yankee race which has made our region a byword for the very best in the American character.

But the representation—the portrait! I struggled to keep a calm face while behind my mask my thoughts clashed and clamored in my skull. How did she dare to display it? Did she realize what it showed? Had she, perhaps, some doubt about it and so kept it here on the landing, half hidden, protected from the glance of the occasional visitor entering the hallway below? And yet did she see in it some vital truth about herself and so choose to display it somewhere, discreetly, instead of banishing it to that attic where reposed the ephemera of her contact with the artist?

Let me describe it. The subject—"Annie!"—was in three-quarter view; her body was seated at right angles to the painter, but her head was turned full face. I have seen—you have seen—many poses like it; it is a favorite stance of both artist and subject. Almost invariably, however, the model's eyes—the focal point of the composition—are directed obliquely away from the viewer. This is especially true of female subjects. I need not digress on the chilling—the very alienating—effect produced by a woman's bold and unwavering stare; and if this is so in life, it is even more so in portraiture, which captures its subject for all time. To have a portrait of a woman—an object meant to soothe, to lighten our days!—ruined by the presence of staring, wuestioning eyes, bold, provocative eyes—eyes

60

that ask answers to questions no woman ought to know—horrible!

I did a rapid calculation. If I figured correctly, Mrs. Richmond must have been about fifty years old when she sat for Hough. He must have been about twenty. I dared not pause to consider the implication of these numbers. The point was that this purported to be the representation of a middle-aged woman—a woman of some place in society, a woman of good family, a woman refined and educated as women are—in short, a gentlewoman.

Gentlewoman! No Haymarket streetwalker ever looked less the part than Mrs. Richmond here. Her dress was pink, and so shockingly low-cut that Lily Langtry herself might have hesitated to wear it. Her arms, too, were bare; and on that expanse of flesh, and on the shoulders and bosom, I saw that the artist had lavished his greatest skill. Man never knew flesh like that in mortal woman! Ah . . . but here—captured forever—he could feast his hungry eyes to satiation!

The mouth curved as if about to speak, or perhaps bestow an ineffable caress? The chin tilted up; a cunning ear peeped from beneath a curl. My eye traveled slowly down the curving lines of the torso to the point where the hands lay loosely in the lap. A white damask rose dangled from the slender fingers of the right hand. And yet, such was the skill of the artist, the rose went almost unnoticed because the eye of the viewer was so strongly directed to the unmistakable curve of the thigh under the supposed cover of pink silk.

I did not know what to say, but obviously I had to say something. I had, startled as I was, to resume my role. I cleared my throat.

"Magnificent!" I said. "Nothing second-rate about it—it is a wonderful likeness."

I smiled; I shook my head; I pretended to examine it all over again. Mrs. Richmond stood calmly, patiently, waiting for me to finish. I was uncomfortably aware of her daughter's presence. At last I felt sufficiently in control to look at her.

I need not have bothered, for she did not look at me. Nor did she examine the portrait, nor yet share an affectionate glance with her mother. Her distress was all too evident. She was visibly writhing with embarrassment—horrible humiliation. She knew what that portrait told; she knew its message, even if her mother did not—or did not choose to.

I wished that we were alone, she and I, so that I might offer her a word of comfort. As it was, I quickly looked away before she raised her eyes to mine, thereby increasing her mortification. Poor daughter! To live in constant view of this blatant exhibition! To pass, a dozen times a day, this vision of all that every decent woman strives to suppress! My heart went out to her; I moved to descend the stairs, and so remove us all from the source of her discomfiture.

We returned to the parlor, I chatting glibly all the while about first- and second-rate talents, et cetera; Mrs. Richmond glibly responding; her daughter trailing silent behind us. The room was as dark as ever; the storm had continued, the wind moaned in the chimney, the sleet had turned to snow. Mrs. Richmond ordered her daughter to light the fire. Soon we sat before its comforting blaze, and, my notebook on my knee, I began at last to get the promised recollections.

Many times that afternoon I thought how happy—how ecstatic—I would have been had the pencil in my hand recorded her other—her so infinitely more valuable—memories. As it was I wrote twenty pages about Henry

Claypool Hough, for now that she had begun she was evidently not to be stopped until the last fragment had been included, the final detail brought forth and dutifully written down. She talked—how she talked! She told me everything. No—not quite. She never mentioned the cartoons. I hardly expected that she would. But certainly—if in fact he had made them—she did not seem to hold it against him. When finally in the late afternoon she paused to receive Triphena bearing the tea tray, I put down my pencil and shook my cramped hand and uttered a rueful laugh.

"This is certainly more than I had hoped to get," I said (more to the daughter than to her mother). "I'll have that book in spite of myself, at this rate!"

Mrs. Richmond handed me my tea. "I had not realized, myself, how much I remembered. One forgets, one goes on. The past fades away."

Unpleasant thought! "On the contrary, dear lady," I replied, "you have made the past more vivid than this moment. You have marvelous recall. It is you who ought to write the book."

"Oh . . . me!" She laughed; she waved her hands at me. Charming! "I can't write anything. I haven't the facility."

"I'm sure you could if you tried," I murmured. I sensed that we were getting rather nearer than she realized to a vastly more exciting topic. "Sometimes one needs just a hint—a little push—the long forgotten slant of light through a window, the smell of lavender from an unused drawer—"

Her expression changed just then; she frowned. No, I thought; surely it cannot be that now she will begin!

"Yes," she said. "Exactly. Do you know, you have just reminded me of something else. How very strange! The smell of—not lavender, but burned meat, if you can imag-

63

ine it! Do you remember" (this to the daughter) "the time when Henry's mother was ill? You weren't more than three or four yourself. We lived on Ames Street then" (this to me) "and Henry and his older sister were trying to manage the house all by themselves, poor little things. And I went over. I took you with me" (this to the daughter) "thinking you could play with him while I tended to Mrs. Hough, and when we opened the door we were overpowered—simply overcome!—by that smell! The meat had burned dry. It took days to get the odor out of the house. Henry always said afterwards that he wanted to try to paint that smell, but I don't suppose he ever did."

My hand had stopped trembling; I scribbled a brief note. Not yet!

The clock on the mantel struck five. I had not been aware of the time before that moment. I took a piece of pound cake; as I ate it—delicious!—I wrestled with my latest dilemma. Mrs. Richmond had been more than kind; she had spent far more time with me than I would have had any right to expect even had I been what she thought I was. Now, however, I had not only to take leave of her (I could hardly impose any longer that afternoon), I had to invent some new excuse to return. For all her gossip about Hough, I sensed in her—no less than in her daughter—a certain reticence, a refusal to be pressed. No—the introduction of that other name had to be made at a far more propitious moment than had yet occurred. Ideally it would come first from her. I would pretend surprise, interest, devotion—she would see my complete sincerity—and at last I would have what I sought. But how? Every passing moment made my presence more ill-mannered; I had to go, and yet I could not go without the means to return.

Again it was the daughter who saved me. Realizing my predicament (and, no doubt, enjoying it), she walked to

64

the window and looked out into the darkness. I am sure she saw nothing; and yet, turning, she said, "The snow is quite deep. How do you plan to get back to town? For that matter, how did you come?"

"I took the horsecars to . . . what is it, Nesmith Street?"

"Sometimes they do not run during storms."

I do not think, now, that she realized then what she was doing. She was—simply—bored; I was a temporary diversion. I thought that then; despite everything, I think it now.

Mrs. Richmond went to the window, too, and then she went out into the hall and opened the front door. In a moment she was back.

"It is very bad. You will freeze just walking to the stop, and very likely they won't be running."

Of course I saw what must happen. I made my feeble protest (which they expected) in order that they might make an even stronger protest (which now I expected) in reply.

After a moment it was settled, not, I think, too awkwardly. I could not, after all, have anticipated the blizzard; we were, all of us, at the mercy of the elements, and if these two women chose to extend their own mercy to me, why, then, I would be a fool not to accept it.

I had paid my bill at the hotel that morning, having determined as I left that if I needed to stay in the city for another night or two, I would find a quieter, more agreeable place. I had left behind the few cheap things I had bought, but no matter. They had kept, it seemed, some of the late Mr. Richmond's toilet articles and nightclothes. These they directed Triphena to put into a back bedroom. Mrs. Richmond informed us that she was going to lie down before dinner. It was left to her daughter, therefore, to take a lamp and matches from the sideboard and show me upstairs.

As she led the way (past that unspeakable portrait!) she said nothing and I followed both her and her example. I did not care for what she might have said—what she might have thought; it was enough that I was so much further along in my plan, and that now, surely, as a guest in their house, I would swiftly and certainly find my way to what I sought.

We paused at the door to the room assigned to me; she opened it and handed the unlit lamp to me and waved me inside, saying that she, too, wanted to retire to rest a while.

I thought, then, to make some small effort to show her that I bore her no ill will for all her help to me that day, whatever its motive. It occurred to me that I did not yet know her Christian name. I smiled at her; I asked her what it was.

Although a gas jet flickered high in the front of the upstairs hall, here in back, where we stood, the light was very dim. And so if there was any expression—anything!—on her face, in her eyes, as she answered me, I did not see it.

I saw only the movement of her lips; I heard her speak the single word:

"Lenore."

8

OUR TACIT agreement that afternoon had been that I would stay the night. But on the morrow, as I worked at fashioning myself to their routine, Mrs. Richmond remarked that on the day following she would find some further item for me which needed Triphena to hunt it out. Triphena that day was baking and not to be disturbed; therefore I would have the thing on the next. So easily was I settled in; so easily did they make me a part of their lives.

By the end of my first full day in their house we had set the pattern for many—not all!—of the days to follow. In the mornings we arose at eight o'clock and had breakfasted by nine. Then, as Mrs. Richmond tended to her personal affairs—whatever they were—I was ensconced in the parlor with the growing dossier on Hough. Except for the presence of the household cat, a large Tabby, I was alone these hours. Triphena went about her work, and the daughter, too, seemed to have some occupation which kept her busy until lunch.

I say "the daughter." I must attempt to use, now, that name which came, later, so easily to my lips but which, for the first day or two, seemed so unbearably awkward. Lenore! I had never known anyone so named; neither, I suspected, had he. It was a name for a poem only—not something with which to address an individual who seemed so far from the poet's romantic ideal of womanhood. Lenore! "Rare and radiant maiden," indeed!

As she sat across from me at meals I wondered what he would have said about her. Would he have been angered by the bestowal of the name upon so prosaic a specimen of that sex which he so professed to love? Or would he have been heartened by his Annie's attempt to have a constant reminder of him at her side? (Here a startling thought came to me, but I put it by, reminding myself to check the city's birth records at the earliest possible moment.)

Through that first night in my room at the rear of the house I slept my troubled sleep and awakened several times, wondering where I was, and I was sure that my restlessness was in no small part a result of the shock of that name. It was not a perfectly comfortable chamber, although it was somewhat larger than my place at the hotel and considerably better furnished. The bedstead, table, washstand and chiffonier were of maple, factory-made, in the plain country style. A handsome patch quilt covered the bed. On the floor was a serviceable braided rug; the walls were papered in a pale floral pattern. Although I was not absolutely sure, I surmised that the window faced north, across the river valley; the next morning, surveying the prospect, I saw that I had been correct.

All of this sounds pleasant enough; but on that first night, on that first occasion when I stepped across the threshold, literally staggering from the shock of "Lenore," I sank down onto the somewhat lumpy bed and after a moment, putting a match to the lamp, looked about me and felt a positive chill.

I do not mean that the room was cold, although, lacking a fireplace, it was hardly warm. No—it was a chill whose source was not so easily discovered; it was a chill which seemed to emanate not from any particular point, but to be a part of the room itself. It was a chill which, I thought, would not be dispelled by any amount of flame or even by central heating. It came from the walls, the floor, the very furniture itself, and was altogether a more palpable thing than the stale, slightly cold musty air which is present in any sealed-off chamber.

I sat on the bed that night and digested the fact of "Lenore," and reassured myself with the thought of what a tremendous distance I had come in the last forty-eight hours. Much farther, I thought, than the thirty miles from Boston—much farther than the mile or two from the center of the city to this residential hill. I had come—yes!—to the very threshold of success. I needed now only to watch my step and so go easily across.

I looked then at the small pile of toiletries which Triphena had placed on the washstand. The razor was slightly discolored along the edge, as if someone had not dried it carefully, and the pot of shaving soap had crusted around the rim. The strop was stiff with age but still serviceable. The silver-backed hairbrush was clean enough, but the bristles were badly worn. From this fact I deduced that Mr. Richmond must have been nearly bald, for surely a man with a full head of hair—a man like me—would find little use for such a brush. The flannel nightshirt and blue woolen dressing gown lay neatly folded on the bed; they were worn but clean, and I thought that the nightshirt at least would be more comfortable than the one which I had purchased in town. Altogether it seemed as if I would do nicely here for the brief duration of my visit.

I looked around me again; simply to change my point of view I sat at the writing table by the window. Seen from this angle, the room looked somehow larger; I could not tell why, but I was comforted by the fact of it. I hate small rooms.

It occurred to me to wonder whose room this might have been. It did not seem sufficiently grand for, say, another Richmond offspring, assuming that there had been one. Had there been, at one time, a poor relation staying here—an orphaned cousin, say, or a maiden aunt? No matter. It would house me well enough.

An idea came to me just then. I sat for a moment, considering it, listening to the wind rattling the panes and beating the snow against the glass. I peered into the shadowed corners. I remained quite still. I allowed my thought to ripen to the point where I could act upon it. I wanted to do nothing hasty, nothing untoward, and yet this little time alone before I met my hostesses again seemed a splendid opportunity to test my powers of ratiocination.

Of course I did not expect to find here what I sought. That would have been too easy, too obvious, and certainly too embarrassing, for if they were secreted here they would be just that—secreted, hidden safely away, not to be found save by the most diligent exploration. And then how would I explain the fact that I had come upon them? I would have to say nothing, continue my charade about Hough, and simply leave the next day or the day after, carrying the treasure away with me. I would, in short, have to steal them.

I did not want to do that. I was, after all, brought up as a

70

gentleman, and although all my near relations are dead, I have still my family's honor to maintain.

Nevertheless, I told myself, a little practice run, here, alone, would not hurt. It would help to pass the time.

Accordingly I began. First I quickly checked the drawers of the chiffonier—nothing, of course—and then I felt underneath the mattress. I felt the mattress itself for a telltale bulge. I ran my palms along the walls, feeling for a weak spot in the plaster, a loose flap of wallpaper. I rolled back the rug and walked carefully across the floor, testing with each step for a loose board.

All this took perhaps half an hour, and at the end of that time I had not discovered anything except a fair amount of dust. I realized how foolish I must look. I smiled at my image in the small mirror over the washstand. Patience!

I stretched out upon the bed. It was not uncomfortable—softer, certainly, than most beds he had had.

And in his final sleep, in the cemetery at Baltimore—did he rest easily there under the monument which had not been erected until more than a quarter of a century after his death, so unimportant was his memory to his countrymen? I wondered if Mrs. Richmond had seen his grave. I promised myself to steer the conversation towards travel—Southern travel.

My eyes grew heavy. I fell into a half doze from which, a short time later, I was aroused by the dinner bell.

* * *

As I have said, we quickly fell into a routine. That first night, after dinner, Mrs. Richmond decreed that we would read aloud. We did—for two hours. We took turns. She had a light and pleasing voice, given to affecting little tremolos at the appropriate times (we were, that night,

71

reading from the *Twice-Told Tales*). The daughter— Lenore—had a somewhat harsher inflection but altogether, I thought, a better sense of the rhythm of the language. I watched her as she read. Her body rested easily on the sofa; she did not sit awkwardly, tentatively, the way so many women do—possibly because she wore no lacings underneath her plain dress? The curve of her cheek, illuminated by the fire, seemed softer than before. She seemed, now, to be one of those women who interest a man not for what they are, but for what they might be. Really, I thought, if only someone would have taken her in hand—someone knowledgeable in the mysteries of the feminine art of disguise, rearrangement, transformation—she would have been a creditable adornment on any man's arm.

When my time came I acquitted myself well enough, although I was bothered by an annoying tickle in my throat which prevented me from expressing the fullest power of the words. However—most important—Mrs. Richmond seemed pleased with me.

The next day I studied alone in the morning; after lunch Mrs. Richmond talked again at length and I filled fifteen pages more in my notebook. That evening we read from a volume of stories by Miss Jewett: pale, inconsequential things, easily read and as easily forgotten.

On the day following I was presented with the promised papers which Triphena had at last found time to unearth. They proved to be not so interesting as Mrs. Richmond had thought. They were letters to Hough from various admirers, kept by his sister and willed by her on her death to Mrs. Richmond. They were almost all conventional expressions of admiration and encouragement, with very little in one to distinguish it from another. However, since Triphena had gotten them for me at her mistress' command, I was voluble in my appreciation to both of them, and I spent somewhat more time going over them than I might otherwise have done.

This task occupied most of the morning of my second full day. That afternoon I had more conversation with Mrs. Richmond; that evening we read Miss Jewett again. All that day I had been turning over in my mind the problem of how I was to extend my fallacious purpose until I could announce my real one. Mrs. Richmond had given me no opportunity in her fluent conversation to introduce the subject of my desire; her daughter—Lenore—had been virtually monosyllabic, expending her voice only in the evening's recitations of the words of others.

But on that evening—that second evening of Miss Jewett—Mrs. Richmond saved me as her daughter—Lenore—had saved me earlier. She decided that there were yet things that I had not seen—things that she could not place; they were probably in the attic, she said; she didn't know. She hadn't looked for relics of Hough for years. In a moment she had decided that the next morning she and I would explore the attic together. Triphena had her work, Lenore (Mrs. Richmond did not refer to her by name) had whatever—the two of us would search alone, therefore, to make absolutely sure that we had overlooked nothing.

My heart, which had been heavy with concern about successfully continuing my charade, immediately rose. Surely—surely—what I really sought was in that attic! And surely, in our search for mementos of Hough, we would—accidentally?—discover it.

I say "accidentally," for it had occurred to me, puzzling over our situation, that it was possible that Mrs. Richmond was perfectly well aware of the reason for my visit—either because she had guessed, or because Lenore had told her.

And it was further possible, I thought, that she was incapable of bringing up the matter on her own—that she was shy, let us say, or perhaps afraid of the effect on her aged heart of looking again at those letters which once, I was sure, had given her all her reason to live. And yet—possible, too—perhaps she wanted me to have them; perhaps she recognized my sincerity, my diligence. Perhaps she now was searching for a natural and easy way to introduce them and so divert me from the lesser man.

But all of this was speculation. The most reasonable theory was that which I had decided upon before: She was a lonely old woman who was looking for a way to keep an entertaining stranger in her home for a few days more.

And so we searched the attic together the next day. It proved to be a double disappointment. Nothing more of Hough came to light, and nothing either—not a scrap! not a word!—of *him*.

I saw, as we descended the stairs, that we both had our little problem. Really, had I been in the proper mood, I would have laughed at the comedy of our mutual double bind—she thinking how to keep me on in my lie (supposing it to be the truth), and I thinking how to tell the truth without being dismissed as a liar. It seemed to me that day that her attitude toward me had somewhat changed; she seemed—really for the first time—seriously to consider me. She had taken me on so readily; she had given me so much. Was she only now beginning to question her judgment? Or was she subjecting me to a final scrutiny before she took the irrevocable step—before she gave me her treasure?

She seemed slightly distracted at dinner that evening. Perhaps elderly women often seem so. I have little experience of them; I do not know. But her attention wandered from the subject of our conversation (we were discussing the Exposition at Chicago), and several times, after engaging in an exchange with Lenore, I turned to include her in my remarks only to discover her luminous eyes resting upon me and yet—odd sensation—not seeming really to see *me*. Then she would blink and frown and come back to us, as it were; where, I wondered, had she been?

As we proceeded into the parlor afterwards she walked slowly to the bookshelf (the volume from which we had been reading lay upon the table) and ran her fingers lightly over the spines. We awaited her by the fire, deferring to her whim as one always defers to the eldest. Her wandering hand stopped; her fingers rested on a particular book. She seemed to have fallen into a kind of dream. I was a little nervous; I did not like to speak to Lenore and so break whatever spell seemed to have captured Mrs. Richmond, and yet I was beginning to feel the strain of watching constantly for the proper moment to unburden my heart. I felt uncomfortable; something got into my throat. I coughed.

Lenore—stolid, inscrutable Lenore—made no reaction. But Mrs. Richmond started badly, and instantly I opened my mouth to apologize and just as instantly checked my voice. To speak would have been to draw attention to her discomfiture, which I did not want to do, and so I spread my parted lips into a foolish grin and scratched at a nonexistent itch on my neck.

I was lucky; Mrs. Richmond did not seem to mind having been disturbed. She nodded at me in a friendly way. "You should take care to wear something warm. This house is unbearably drafty. We do want to keep you in good health!"

I assured her that my health was perfect. She accepted the assurance with a smile. The awkward moment had passed. She came now to join us. I had put out my hand to pick up Miss Jewett's stories, but then I saw that she had taken a book from the shelf. She held it with both hands, as if, held with only one, it might slip from her grasp and fall to the floor where—so carefully she held it!—it would surely break into a thousand pieces.

I could not see the title. It was a fairly thick volume—about an inch—and its purple cover was badly worn. She looked at us. She looked down at it.

"I think, if you do not mind, that we will read something else this evening. I am not disposed to the literal." She looked up at me—full at me! "Are you," she said slowly, "are you fond of the tales and poems of the author of 'Annabel Lee?'"

9

You can imagine my sensations at that moment. It is not possible for a human being to control the embarrassing rush of blood to his face, but if ever a human tried to do so, it was I at that instant. Naturally I did not succeed. I must have looked a fool, standing awkwardly there, beet red (Why "beet?" It is not the right color), stammering out God knew what reply. I dared not look at Lenore; I hardly dared look at Mrs. Richmond.

"Why—yes, I am," I said, as calmly as I could. "I like him very much."

"Good!" said Mrs. Richmond briskly. "Then we shall have him tonight. We will begin with the tales, I think, and save the poetry for later. We can go round robin, if you like, each picking favorites."

She seated herself; we followed; and she began to read "The Masque of the Red Death." It was fortunate indeed,

I thought, that she had not asked me to begin, for my voice would have betrayed me even as my trembling hands threatened to do. I folded my arms, I tilted my head in an attitude of rapt attention, I hid my hands under my unbuttoned coat.

As the plot of the story unfolded, I wondered what had led Mrs. Richmond to choose that particular tale. Prince Prospero and his friends were shut away from the world as she herself appeared to be. Did she see perhaps a resemblance? But what Death stalked her here?—except of course that inevitable, natural sleep which comes to us all at the end of our lives.

Lenore read next—"The Pit and the Pendulum." And then it was my turn. Although I was of course thoroughly familiar with all his work, I was for a moment at a loss to pick. I found to my dismay that I could not remember the plots, and I did not want to choose something awkward that would perhaps send Mrs. Richmond weeping to bed. No. The door had opened, it had been opened—as I had seen it must be—by her, not me, and I wanted now to do nothing to slam it shut. In the end I read "The Cask of Amontillado," followed by Mrs. Richmond with "The Oblong Box" and Lenore with "A Tale of the Ragged Mountains." Then I read "The Man of the Crowd," agonizing all over again with the nameless protagonist as he roamed the hostile city.

At that point Mrs. Richmond turned to the poems and I relaxed a little. I had feared that she might be so daring as to read "Landor's Cottage," and I very much dreaded the effect of that idyll upon us. But we were saved—whether by her good sense or her timidity I did not know—and she gave us a spirited "Bells." Of course the poems, too, had their dangers—would I hear, tonight, "For Annie" read by the woman to whom it was addressed? And what about "Lenore?" Would they expect from me a comment on the daughter's name—so unusual a name that its bestowal surely could not have been a coincidence? But we made the perilous voyage safely, I with "Dream-Land," Mrs. Richmond with "Annabel Lee," Lenore with "Israfel," I with "Eldorado." At last we heard the clock strike ten. Mrs. Richmond closed the book. She smiled at us.

"That was . . . very nice," she said. "Very nice indeed. There is no one quite like him, I think, in all of literature."

She stood up; she returned the book to its place. She said good night. Lenore and I rose and saw her out and then, as if by mutual, although unspoken, consent, we sat again and hesitated for a moment, assaying each other like pugilists before their combat. The fire burned low, radiating a soothing warmth; save for an occasional snapping spark, the house was very quiet. We could not hear Mrs. Richmond moving about on the floor above.

Finally I could contain myself no longer. The evening just past—in his company!—had been an unbearable strain on my nerves; I was more anxious than ever to see those other words which he had written, phrases—whole pages! In his own hand! Unpublished!

"Does she know?" I demanded, more fiercely than I had intended.

Lenore remained infuriatingly calm. "Know what?"

"Don't play about. Does she know the truth?"

"About you?"

"Of course about me. Does she know what I want? Have you told her?"

She raised her eyebrows at me; she even smiled a little, very wry. "I have told her nothing. We rarely converse, my mother and I. I learned long ago never to confide in her. You see for yourself how she talks."

"Then why did we read *him* tonight? Do you think she has guessed?"

"She may have. I told you—I don't know."

I bit my lips in vexation. Really, she was maddening! "What do you think she would say if I went to her now— no, tomorrow—and confessed?"

"Everything?"

"Everything. If I threw myself on her mercy, begged her to help me, convinced her of my sincerity—"

Higher and higher went her eyebrows. "After four days of lies?"

"Yes! She will understand; she will grant the worth of my motives, at least. What would my chances be?"

She appeared to consider my question; she looked away into the low-burning embers. At last she said, "I think she would deny you—evict you on the spot."

"No!" It was too painful; I could not bear it.

"Yes."

"Why? When she has been so kind about the other—"

"She doesn't care about him. He never touched her heart. It does not hurt to give away what we do not value."

True, true—but I could not accept it. I had to try—

She looked at me as if she expected me to say something more. When I did not, she said, "Will it pain you very much?"

"To fail?"

"Yes."

I made a brave show. "I do not expect to fail. She is a good woman, my experience these past days proves it. She will help me."

"By giving you what you want?"

"Yes."

She shook her head. "She will never do that."

"She must! She could not be so cruel as to keep them from me when she sees how devoted I am—"

"You forget that your devotion is nothing compared to

80

hers. She knew him before you were born. Her devotion is older than you yourself."

I could think of no rebuttal, and so I was silent. I looked away; I looked around the shadowed room. I stared, finally, into the fire. What was I to do? Had I come so far only to fail? There must—there *must* be a way.

But of course there was. I felt my growing agitation. I put my hand on her arm; I pressed her flesh. Despite the covering sleeve of brown serge, I felt her warmth.

"Listen. Will you help me?"

She did not withdraw her arm.

"Help you?"

"Yes. Will you?"

"To do what?"

"To get them."

"What do you mean? Take them? Steal them?"

I winced at her choice of words. "To . . . to take them, yes; but do not call it stealing to put them into my care. This is an act of devotion, after all, not larceny. Will you help me?"

"How?"

"I do not know. We must find them—somehow! Where do you imagine they might be?"

She stared at me.

"Think! Has she ever . . . ever . . . mentioned them? Has she ever shown special concern for any part of this house, any place where she might have hidden them? She must have said something during all these years! It is impossible that they should be here and you not know—"

In my excitement I gripped her arm more tightly. She suddenly pulled away with a little cry of pain, but so intent was I on convincing her to help me that I did not think to apologize.

81

"When did you move into this house?"

"Some years after the war—eighteen seventy-one."

"Your—ah—father was alive?"

"Yes."

"And surely your mother would have wanted to keep them hidden from him?"

"Yes."

"And so on the day you moved—on the day the vans brought the furniture—your mother would have been here, searching for a place to hide them. A loose floorboard, a warped panel—"

"There were no loose boards. My father supervised the construction of the house; he often remarked on how well built it was."

"A trunk, then, brought from your former home, a desk with a hidden drawer—"

"No. There is nothing like that. I would know of it." She smiled her wry smile again. "I was an inquisitive child. Nothing remained hidden from me."

"But they did. You never found them."

"Unless—"

"What?"

"Unless they do not exist at all."

I did not at once take her meaning. "Do not exist! But they must! They must exist. They must be here . . . ah, do not say *that*! Ingram published some of them. She had them then; she showed them to him!"

"She made copies for him—selectively, I believe. But I was not here. I was still at school. I am sure that she had no witness as she worked, and I am equally sure that no one ever saw the letters themselves."

"Nevertheless, they existed then. And if she had them then, she has them now."

"Has it occurred to you that she may have destroyed them?"

"You cannot believe that. You have said yourself that she would never let me have them. You would not have spoken so if you thought she—burned them, or discarded them somehow." I shuddered; I could not bear to think of such a catastrophe.

She appeared to consider my argument. I saw then that she had thrown up her last feeble defense against me; and, seeing it immediately overcome, that she was ready now to listen to my importunations.

"No," she said at last. "I would not." She gazed upon me; we both understood that for the moment at least I had won. I hurried on to strike the final blow.

"Help me."

"When?"

"Now—tonight."

For a moment still she hesitated. Then, in a voice so low that I had to strain to hear, she said, "Very well."

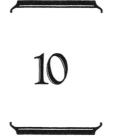

10

I HAD imagined an arduous expedition on hands and knees under the low-lying roof in a corner of the attic, or—worse still—a descent into the cellar where, fighting off hordes of vermin, we would chip away at whitewashed earthen walls until we discovered the secret cache.

The reality proved to be much less repugnant. Lenore, after those two welcome words of assent, pushed back her chair and went unhesitatingly to the bookcase where, not half an hour before, her mother had placed the volume from which we had read. She beckoned me to her side; she knelt in front of the shelves and without further invitation I crouched beside her. The light was very poor here, but sufficient for our purposes.

"I am going to explain this to you," she said, "and then I am going to leave you here alone. I would ask you to consider what you do. I would ask you to look at them, to copy them if you must, but do not take them away. Leave them here for her. She is an old woman, she has not long to live—do not break her heart by stealing them."

I agreed—I would have agreed to anything! With mounting excitement I watched her strong capable hands range over the elaborately carved bottom panel—a panel perhaps five inches high between the floor and the bottom shelf.

"You would be interested to know," she said, "that Henry Hough built these shelves for my mother before he left for Europe. He was very handy—a craftsman. She gave him specific directions, of course. My father was pleased at Hough's gift; he never suspected the reason for the bottom panel."

A secret spring—of course! And within the hiding place—the treasure! My heart near choked me as I watched her press and prod, searching for the sensitive spot lying somewhere on the whorled and convoluted surface. I could not believe that in a moment's time I would have them in my hands—that I would read his words, see his pen marks, the flourish of his name!

"Ah!" She had found it. The panel slid across to reveal the space within. But even as I reached out to seize the contents (which I could not see, but which I was sure lay waiting), she pushed it shut again. The faint *click!* of the panel as it slid into place on its spring might have been the click of a pistol aimed at my head, so final, so fatal a sound it was.

I could not help but remonstrate. "Why did you do that? Do you want me to collapse completely? You know how I long to see them!"

She stood up; she shook her skirts into place.

"I have given you the key," she said, looking down at me. "I do not need to stay and watch the theft. I am going to bed now. What you do here after I have gone is none of

86

my affair. But remember—I trust you not to hurt her. You are on your honor."

She left me alone. I heard her rather heavy tread ascend the stairs; then nothing, total silence.

Like the lover who purposely extends the agonizing moments before the achievement of his deepest, most passionate desire, I held back then, kneeling in front of that panel. I did not touch it; I waited, fairly calm, prolonging the delicious pain of my anticipation. Finally I put out my hand; I touched the polished wood. I felt its smoothness, its deep carvings, I imagined it as it must have been before Hough fashioned it. I began to press, my trembling fingers sought the place, I pushed, hard—

Nothing happened. I tried again. Still the panel refused to move. I began to perspire most unpleasantly. Repeatedly I pressed the spot; then I pressed around it, an inch away, two inches—

Nothing. I gave it a final, vicious prod and so threw myself off balance. I fell back, I sat down hard on the floor and almost cried out at the sharp pain reverberating up my spine.

"What are you doing?"

Her words struck at my heart and shriveled it. I felt myself prepare to die. Somehow I found the courage to turn my head, to look—

No, it was not a ghost, although it—she—might have been, so still she stood, so—*white!* I shut my eyes.

"Answer me!"

I opened them; I looked. Not a ghost. A live figure stood there—Annie Richmond. Her hair tumbled down around her shoulders, her frail old body was enveloped in a billowing white cover—a sheet?—her face, distorted with anger, was paler even than her shroud. But she was very much alive, very definitely flesh and blood.

She came at me. Painfully I stood up.

87

"You! You—*biographer!*" Her eyes blazed (it is the only word), strings of spittle hung from her contorted lips. An avenging Fury would not have been so frightening a vision as Annie Richmond at that moment; certainly I was frightened. Terrified!

Of course I had to say something. But I was able to get out only a single word—"Please!"—before my throat constricted and I felt bitter tears burn my eyes. All my strength had gone; I was weak, hardly able to stand.

She halted by the table; through my tears I saw that she, too, was trembling. "'Please' what, you thief! Look at you! You are as miserable a specimen as I have seen—and I have seen many, I assure you. I never really trusted you. I should have known better, I should have followed my original instinct and shut you out in the beginning. Henry Hough, indeed!"

It must be remembered that I had been under the severest strain for almost a week; that I had endured the train, the hotel, strange and lumpy beds, indifferent food; that my nerves were stretched tight on the rack of my compulsion. Only thus can I explain my actions; only thus can I make clear that what I did, I did from impulse rather than design.

I sank on my knees before her. I covered my weeping eyes with my hands. I bent low until my forehead touched her unshod feet. Had she kicked me, beaten me, I would not have minded; she could have done what she pleased at that moment, and I would not have held her actions against her. I wanted only to assuage her anger; I wanted only to be allowed to stay.

There was a long silence. We remained frozen in our wretched little tableau. Then, as if from a very great distance, I heard her voice again. It was a different voice—

still hard, still unfriendly, but the anger had gone. My heart began to revive.

"What an extraordinary young man you are."

I could think of no reply. Slowly I lifted my head; I uncovered my face.

"Do you not understand what it is you deal with here?" she said. "You are not seeking the mindless jottings of some anonymous traveler who wrote a duty letter once a month to his family! You are not even seeking specimens of mere literary merit—travel letters, say, written by a literate journalist—are there any such? No! You understand what I say to you? You are seeking—you are trying to steal—*his* letters! Words of genius! Immortal lines!"

I nodded. Still I had no answer.

"Do you know what that means? To me, it means that you suffer from a very serious problem."

I groaned an assent.

"And do you know what that problem is?"

I shook my head.

"Conceit!"

I glanced up sharply at her then. Impudent old woman!

"Yes! Conceit—pure self-concern!" She stared down at me triumphantly. "Who on earth do you think you are, that you can come in here all unannounced, no credentials whatever, no introduction, and simply take what I hold dearest in all the world?"

Odd—some women speak so of their children.

As if she read my mind she said quickly, maliciously,

"Why do you not try to take my daughter? I would let you have *her*, absolutely!"

I have found that a glimpse of humor in one's opponent is always a sign of weakness. Therefore, at that point, I stood up. I realized at once that being slightly taller than she gave me, if not an advantage, at least a lesser handicap. She understood. She looked down. When after a moment she spoke again, I realized—yes!—that her voice now was the voice which *he* must have heard. Its beguiling, caressing tone excited me more than I can say.

"You are very cruel to break an old woman's heart."

"Dear madam—"

"Yes! Very cruel." She looked full at me.

O coquette! O temptress! The eyes alone remained from that former self; all else was age, decay, a preparation for the grave.

I did not care to discuss my cruelty; I carried the attack into her camp.

"You are not old."

Wordlessly she lifted between two fingers a strand of her snow-white hair.

"No—you are not! Annie Richmond can never be old. She will live forever young."

"As he knew her." She touched her cheek with the back of her hand. Her eyes looked beyond me; she went, just for a moment, to a far place where I could not follow.

I waited. When she came back she was my enemy no more. And if she was not yet the friend she had been, she seemed at least to have reached a kind of truce. Her anger had disappeared entirely.

I half expected her to hold out her hand. She did not do that; but she did nod and murmur "Good night," and bestow upon me a most affecting glance before she went away.

And I? What did I do? Did I return at once to the panel and try again to open it? Did I resolve to have—that night—the papers which I had so long desired?

I did not. I poked the fire, I turned down the gas jets, I extinguished the lamp, I shut the door behind me and

90

went upstairs to bed. There were, after all, limits of bad manners beyond which I refused to go. Now that she understood my purpose, I would deal with her openly; I would not try to deceive her again. In the morning, I thought, we will have it out, we will speak our honest thoughts, we will strike a bargain. In the meantime I would rest; I would strengthen myself for the contest to come.

It was not until I had crawled into my chilly bed and had begun to fall asleep that I thought to wonder why—how—I had been discovered. Mrs. Richmond had commented more than once on the soundness of her sleep; she had said (much to my distress!) that a tramp burglar could break into the house any night and steal everything without once awakening her. What, then, had awakened her this night?

And then I saw—the vision haunted me through my dreams—I saw the daughter's face, I heard her words, I saw her as she had looked when she left me alone to struggle with the implacable wood.

Someone, in the precious moments I had wasted, had awakened Mrs. Richmond. Someone had alerted her to the danger in the room beneath her own. Perhaps—awful thought!—perhaps that same someone whose name I knew so well had listened outside the door as Mrs. Richmond confronted me.

We must, I thought, have pleasured her immensely. Nausea overwhelmed me as I contemplated her enjoyment of my defeat.

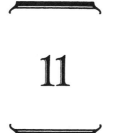

11

THE MORNING brought new hope, as mornings always do, and as I shaved and dressed and tidied myself I hummed a cheerful tune and even smiled at my reflection in the glass. I am not a handsome man, but I am present-able enough. Certainly my countenance exhibits none of those tendencies toward weakness and dissipation which so disfigure many bachelors—men like me—of indepen-dent means and interminable leisure. I have had an easy and pleasant life. Born to good family, reared with every advantage, I have traveled, I have lived well. I have had the best that the world can offer. My face reveals this fact. Further, I go clean-shaven, and so look somewhat younger than I am. My hair is dark, my forehead broad and high with marked development at the temples. My nose is fine and straight, my mouth full without being overly sensu-ous. My best feature, I have been told, is my eyes. They are deep-set, brown, rather heavy-lidded, but their long dark lashes give them grace, and the good mind behind them (if I may say so) provides the intelligence so necessary to any pleasing expression.

My pocket watch showed the hour to be not yet eight o'clock when I finished my toilet. Triphena invariably served meals precisely on time; I did not care to go down early and possibly be forced to make conversation with either Mrs. Richmond or her daughter before we had been awakened by our coffee. This morning of all mornings I wanted no awkward moment with nothing to do except struggle with our awareness of each other without the helpful accouterments of cups and plates, porridge bowls and trays of ham and eggs.

My room lacked reading materials. I sat by the window, therefore, and gazed at the truly magnificent view which it afforded. Brilliant sun sparkled on a landscape covered with deep snow. Far below, down the steep cliff, through the tops of bare branches, I saw the black water of the river. Even such bitter cold as we had endured for the past several days had failed to halt that mighty current. It rushed and tumbled toward the sea thirty miles to the east. Directly underneath my window was Mrs. Richmond's small back garden. A long white mound showed the line of the stone wall which marked the edge of the precipice. To my right I saw the corner of the carriage barn and a bit of its unplowed driveway. To my left, farther west up the river valley, I saw the dirty smudge of smoke from the factory chimneys; already, at this early hour, they were in full operation.

I heard a sound outside my door. Instantly I was alarmed—surely she would not visit me now, before breakfast? In three steps I had my hand on the knob. I turned it, I threw open the door.

94

There was no one. I looked down the hall; I thought I glimpsed a figure descending the stairs, but I was too late. Impossible to tell which of the three women it was. Curious—had someone been listening? I knew that I was, now, an object of the gravest suspicion—but what did they hope to learn by eavesdropping on my solitude? Did they think that I spoke to myself, that I talked loudly of my plans to my reflection in the mirror?

I stepped out into the hall—more to listen than to see—and I tripped and just caught myself from falling.

A package lay at the threshold. It was perhaps two feet long by eighteen inches wide, wrapped in brown paper and tied with common twine. A note was tucked under the string. I picked it up and returned to my room, shutting the door behind me. I put the package on the table by the window; I took out the note. But before I read it I puzzled for a moment about what had been delivered to me. Its shapelessness and its sensation in my hands indicated that it was not a box. Whatever it was felt soft, like cloth, and yet heavy—there was a definite weight and solidity to it.

I unfolded the note:

Please wear these at tea today.

No signature; it needed none. One person only gave orders in this household, and despite the "please" this was as much a command as any she gave to Triphena or Lenore.

I slipped off the string, I pulled open the paper. I saw a folded suit of clothes—black. Coat, trousers, vest—even a stock, all black, all in the style of long ago—fifty years at least. I had never seen a living person in clothing such as these. I had seen them only in portraits.

I have said just now that my eyes reflected some intelligence; but my brain was functioning poorly that morning,

95

for it was a full five minutes at least before I understood. I lifted the coat; I held it up. It seemed about my size. The trousers, too, seemed the proper length. I slipped off my own dark jacket and tried on the other. It fit. Odd! I wrapped the stock loosely around my neck, over my collar. I did not like it; it made me feel as if I were being choked. Very odd! I removed the stock and coat; I examined everything again. They were, I saw now, badly worn, although they seemed clean. The jacket cuffs were frayed, the material at the elbows was quite thin. I looked at the note once more. What was she about?

And then all of a sudden I realized her plan. My knees went weak; I sat down in the chair too hard and gasped at the pain in my lower spine.

My brain struggled to comprehend. I thought of Mrs. Richmond's actions, of her words to me, for the past three days. Her mood had swung from anger to cordiality to real sympathy and back to anger again—followed by, I thought, a kind of cautious acceptance at the very last. At no time had she given any indication of mental instability—of insanity, if you will. Many elderly people, living out their lives removed from the everyday world, probably become mildly eccentric, but she did not seem even that. Her anger had been the anger of a rational person who rebuffs intrusion by a stranger. It had alarmed me, but it had not struck me as being out of character. But this! What was I to make of such a thing? Did she expect me to acknowledge it at breakfast? Did I dare to question her, to argue with her?

I folded the note. I stood up, put on my own coat, and slipped the note into my pocket. I folded the black clothing and put them and the paper and twine into an empty drawer of the bureau. I went out, closing the door behind me, and descended to breakfast.

Although it was now some minutes past eight, neither

Mrs. Richmond nor her daughter was in the dining room. I saw that only one place—mine—was laid. I sat down. I poured my coffee from the silver pot, I removed the covers from the plates of ham, eggs, pancakes; I began to eat. The house was very quiet—I might have been alone. Triphena quite startled me when suddenly she appeared; I almost choked on a piece of meat. She appraised me, waiting for me to recover.

"Good morning, Triphena," I got out at last.

"Morning."

"Where is Mrs. Richmond today? Surely you do not expect me to eat all this food by myself?"

She shrugged. Both of us were aware that it was a matter of total indifference to her what—or how much—I ate. "She isn't coming down," she said.

"I am sorry—is she ill?"

"No. She spends the day in her room sometimes. She gets tired, she rests."

"And Miss Richmond?"

"She went out early."

Ashamed, no doubt, to face me after her nasty trick.

"I see—for the day?"

Again a shrug. "Mrs. Richmond said she'd see you at tea."

Yes—of course. "Thank you, Triphena. Tell her I inquired for her and that I hope she is well."

She acknowledged this instruction with only a slight twitch of her thin, rigid mouth, and without ceremony she began to clear the table. Really, servants can be maddening in their inservility! I refuse to keep them—too often the master becomes the slave.

I wandered into the parlor, which was somewhat brighter than usual on this brilliant morning. Inevitably my eyes were drawn to the carved bottom panel of the bookcase,

97

but I remembered my promise to myself: No longer would I skulk like a common thief. Now that Mrs. Richmond had found me out, I would behave with as much honor as I could manage in the circumstances. I would strike a bargain with her, fair and square. And if she refused me—but that was unthinkable. She must understand the urgency of my need. I must make her understand. I must exert all my powers to influence her.

I went to the bookshelf. Keeping resolutely away from him whose words so greatly excite me, I selected at last a good, safe, moderately engrossing volume—*The Portrait of a Lady*—and settled myself on the sofa. The morning passed pleasantly enough in the company of Isabel Archer, and after lunch—solitary—I returned to her. When at last I saw that it was three thirty, I was reluctant to leave her, and so I took her with me to my room.

I will confess that despite my determination to do anything within reason to attain my objective, I had still quite a little struggle with myself during the next half hour. I got out the funereal suit; I removed my jacket; I took up that poor frayed cloth and held it to me, trying, I suppose, to get from it some reassurance that in obeying Mrs. Richmond's instructions I was furthering my own cause.

At last I removed my trousers and pulled on the black; I took off my coat and vest and put on the black; I removed my tie and wound the smothering stock around my collar. I performed these actions with trembling hands, with heavily beating heart—but I did in fact perform them. Understand that: No one stood over me forcing me to put on that costume. And although it was clear that I was being persuaded to do so—the implication of the package being well understood by me—still I had, in fact, the choice of walking out the door of that house and returning to my own life. That such a choice was unthinkable—that Mrs.

Richmond knew that it was unthinkable—is beside the point.

I stood for a moment in my stark black raiment, trying to get accustomed to my new self. One's clothing is such a personal thing that suddenly to don the costume of another—garments totally unlike one's own—is to suffer a very real shock. I was still myself—and yet I was someone else as well. I was still myself—and yet I looked different, and so I felt different, odd, uncomfortably a stranger within my own skin. I did not dare to look at myself in the mirror. The reflection would be, I thought, too unsettling—it would only further confuse me. What is more, I was afraid that I looked perfectly ridiculous, and a giggle now at my appearance would only have the result of forcing me to put on my own clothing and so, inevitably, to anger Mrs. Richmond once again.

I left my room; I went downstairs. The door of the parlor was closed. I knocked; from within came Mrs. Richmond's voice bidding me to enter.

She sat by the new-lit fire as she had sat every day, the tea things spread before her, the curtains drawn against the dusk, her little world safe enclosing her. She was (I saw, envious) dressed as perfectly as usual; really, I had never seen an old woman so exquisitely turned out. The soft, dove-colored silk of her dress matched her lacy shawl; amethysts glowed at her collar and on her fingers. I stood somewhat awkwardly before her. She took me in, she looked me up and down. There was an expression in her eyes which I could not make out—the satisfaction of a parent, perhaps, whose child does exactly as instructed. She nodded slowly, several times, and then she bade me sit opposite her. She handed me my tea. Still not a word of recognition at what I had done for her came from her lips. I sipped the burning liquid; I stifled my impulse to speak first. The ball was in her court; let her strike it as she would.

Finally she said, "Did you have a profitable day?"

"Pleasant. Hardly profitable."

"What did you do?"

"I read."

"What?"

"*The Portrait of a Lady.*"

She wrinkled her nose. "A little dry, isn't it?"

"No. I enjoyed it."

"He always seems to me to be at one remove from—true experience."

"Perhaps it is simply his style which puts you off."

"Perhaps. It does not matter."

She closed her eyes. She seemed to be concentrating on some inner vision. After a moment, her eyes still closed, she said, "Come here."

I put down my cup; I took a step and stood in front of her.

"Kneel," she said sharply.

I hesitated, cursing my impetuous action of the night before. Finally I did as she commanded.

She opened her eyes, then, and looked down at me. She raised her hand; very lightly she touched my hair. I willed myself not to flinch; my determination not to let her unnerve me was all the more necessary in the next moment when I realized what she was doing.

She was—believe me—rearranging my hair. Her long thin fingers moved swiftly, surely, lifting the strands and pulling them straight across from part to temple.

"You must let it grow," she said softly—and yet there was a strange urgency in her voice, a kind of breathless anticipation. "It does not reach far enough. You must let it grow longer."

She withdrew her hand; she gazed at me. A faint smile showed on her lips. "But as for the rest—very good! It could not be better. You may get up now."

I did so. But I did not sit again in my chair; sitting was the wrong position, I thought, for whatever role I was supposed to play. To forestall my impulse to touch my hair—it tickled; I did not like it arranged so—I thrust my hands to where pockets would have been. But this infernal costume had no pockets and so I clasped my hands behind my back and struck what I hoped was an authoritative pose by the mantel.

Still faintly smiling, she took me in. Only someone who has been the object of such scrutiny can know the torture of it—the desire to run away, to hide, the desperate attempt to keep still and not fidget. I reminded myself again of the sweet victory which lay before me, almost within my grasp. She must have seen something of my misery reflected in my face, for at last she said, very gently, "Humor me. It can do no harm."

"Can it do good, then?"

"Perhaps. Perhaps. You do not know—you cannot— how it touches my heart to see you."

"To see *me?*"

She shrugged. "To see you *so.* You are very like, you know. It is amazing."

My irritation rose like bile in my throat; I swallowed it. "You do me no service, madam, to take me for a fool."

Her eyes widened prettily. "But I do not. Not at all!"

"What then?"

She shook her head. "Please—do not speak. Let me look at you. Let me—simply sit quiet and look. That is not so very much to ask, it it? That cannot hurt you."

I forebore to argue further; I let her have her way with me. I could have walked out, I could have left her—but I did not. I stayed. For fully fifteen minutes—I timed her by the clock—we remained so; and then at last, with a wave of her hand, she dismissed me in a voice so exhausted and yet so undeniably excited that she might have passed just then through an episode of the most violent emotional upheaval.

I fled upstairs, and not a moment too soon. As I reached the second-floor landing I heard the front door open and, peeping down over the balustrade, I saw the shabby figure of Lenore coming in.

I was thankful to have missed her. I would not have wanted her to see me dressed as I was. There are, after all, extremes of humiliation which even the most devoted knight ought not to be forced to endure.

12

You can understand with what feelings of relief—of high anticipation—I descended to dinner a short time later. I had, I thought, behaved very well; now, dressed again in my own familiar clothes, I felt a pleasant sense of having got a distasteful job behind me. I had humored Mrs. Richmond far beyond any reasonable limit. I had now, I thought, only to press home my case to her and I would be gone victorious.

Our conversation at dinner that night was as it had been on all previous nights—fluent, comfortable, entirely superficial. Lenore said nothing of her activities that day, and not by the slightest glance did she seem to inquire of me about the success—or failure—of my search the night before. Afterwards we retired as usual to the parlor and—awkward moment!—took up Miss Jewett once again as if we had never left her. I bridled my impatience, I read as well as I knew how, I reminded myself that my perseverance would be rewarded. And, indeed, when the time came for us to say good night, I thought that my moment had come, for Mrs. Richmond turned to me with glowing beneficence and said, "I have found a special treasure for you."

I could barely restrain myself from clasping her hand in gratitude.

"A memorial tribute," she went on, "collected by some friends only last year. We had intended to publish it, but money is scarce now and we have not yet raised the necessary funds. If it strikes you as anything worthwhile, you might ask the membership of the Boston Art Club if they would care to underwrite it. I will have Triphena leave it here for you in the morning."

My effusions died in my throat. I watched her go, followed by Lenore; I sat alone not three paces from the real treasure—*my* treasure—and tried to understand what she had told me. Surely she could not expect me to continue with Hough, now that she knew the real purpose of my visit! Or was she sincerely confused—had her aging brain forgotten her discovery of me last night, forgotten the parcel of clothing, the little play we had acted out in this very room not six hours before?

I went swiftly to the bookcase; I knelt before the obdurate panel. I pressed and pounded it; I was tempted to take the poker and rip the thing apart. Her treatment of me was beyond endurance. Did she think that I had nothing better to do with my life than dance to her strange tune? I had come here to strike a bargain, not to wait attendance on her senility. The next day, I thought, I would press her to come to terms with me. And if she would not—

No. To fail was unthinkable. I had already closed my

mind to any notion of defeat. I had come too far, now, to go back empty-handed.

I slept soundly that night—surprisingly!—and in the morning I awoke with renewed determination. I *would* win! Once again I was alone all day. After breakfast I glanced hastily through the "memorial tribute"—a poor collection, better left unpublished—and then returned to Isabel Archer. Just before tea I went up to my room to wash my hands and face and comb my hair.

When I descended, she was waiting for me. I put a pleasant expression upon my face and greeted her as charmingly as I knew how. Instantly I saw my error: She was in no mood for *my* greetings.

"Why are you dressed like that?" she said. "Where are—the other things?"

"They are in my room. I did not understand—"

"Go at once. Do not let me see you at tea again dressed as you are now. Go and come back in the proper costume—and do not forget to rearrange your hair."

What choice did I have? You see the difficulty of my position. I had determined to confront her, once for all. But I could hardly plead my case with her if she would not admit me to her presence. I had no choice—I had to play by her rules. I fled upstairs. With trembling hands I made the change. Not ten minutes later I returned to her. Again I greeted her, and this time, after a long look, she spoke graciously to me and handed me my tea. After I had drunk it I felt much better. I had been quite alarmed. She was positively ferocious when she was angry. She handed me a plate of fruit cookies and I took one—mutual gestures of reconciliation. Her eyes rested on me as they had done yesterday—a proud, happy glance.

"Now," she said at last, "we will try a little conversation—nothing difficult, nothing obscure. Perhaps you can begin by telling me about your magazine—your proposed magazine. It will be, I believe you said, something completely new. There has been nothing like it before?"

For a long moment I hesitated. Our eyes looked deep, each into the other's. She seemed to be giving me wordless encouragement, and I—I was a frightened neophyte actor loath to step upon the stage. Finally I heard my voice:

"That is correct. Completely new."

"And you will be able to engage the finest talent to write for you? Aside from yourself, of course."

"I—yes."

"But that is very good! Your name alone would guarantee its success—and with all the others to contribute, you will be assured of a large subscription. You will be the prince of the literati!"

Modestly I inclined my head.

"I like the name you have chosen for it," she continued. "It is elegant—most unusual." She looked at me expectantly; fortunately I was able to respond.

The Stylus.

"It was original with you."

Here I bristled a bit. "Naturally. I do not plagiarize."

"No—of course you do not. You would never have the need." She smiled so sweetly at me—nodding, encouraging—that I began to take heart.

"You won one hundred dollars for 'The Gold-Bug' in eighteen forty-two, did you not?"

"Ah—yes."

"No." She drew back, annoyed. "It was eighteen forty-three."

"I'm sorry. Eighteen forty-three."

"You should have known that."

"Yes."

"You will make me think that you lack—devotion."

106

"That is the one thing above all others that I possess."

"Then you must work. Work!" She sat back in an attitude of exhaustion. "You have done very well. But you are a little awkward still. It is understandable." She nodded at me. All spirit had gone from her now; she was a tired old woman, worn out by her effort. "You may go. I would ask you to—prepare a little. Study. You are quite good in general but you lack the necessary specifics. No matter—I am very pleased. You may go now."

I went. Leaving that shadowed room and passing into the hall and up the stairs was like going from one existence to another. I struggled to acclimate myself. She had said that she was pleased. That was the important thing. My confusion, my awkwardness, my sense of displacement did not matter. She was happy!

When I reached the safety of my room, I had no sooner closed the door than I began swiftly to remove my costume. It was quite five minutes, therefore, until, dressed again as myself, I saw that I had been given another "present"—a set of books lay neatly stacked on the table. I approached them. Without touching them I examined their titles. But of course I already knew. She had given me—for the "specifics"——Ingram's *Works* and Woodberry's *Life.*

13

I MADE good use of my time on the following day and by four o'clock I had read a good portion of the *Life* and refreshed my memory of the major stories and poems. No more mistakes! I went down to the parlor—properly dressed—precisely on the hour. We greeted each other this day with an ease previously lacking, like actors who are finally at home in their roles. She bade me sit, she gave me tea, she spoke the cue lines for which, today, I had all my replies prepared.

Everything went splendidly for a good while. I produced for her approval fact after authoritative fact—dates, names, titles, plots—and she heard me out with increasing satisfaction. Now, she seemed to be saying, now you have got it! Once or twice, when she scrabbled in the back recesses of her memory to pull out a particularly obscure item, I was even able to anticipate her and give the answer before she put the question. In the matter of the Balloon-Hoax, for example, I pointed out to her the most subtle, most cunning stroke which unquestionably accounted for the success of the deception—that is, that the voyage across the Atlantic, as recounted exclusively in the *New York Sun,* was an *accident*: Mr. Monck Mason and his fellow aëronauts had intended to float only from Wales to Paris, but were caught up in a wayward eastern draught and so conveyed across an ocean instead of a channel. Had the "voyage" been presented as intentionally transatlantic, I declared, its account would not have rung half so true.

She did not spoil our play by commenting explicitly on my erudition; rather, she assumed that fond, proud expression and ever so slightly inclined her head to show that she acknowledged my point. How elegant she was! How accomplished! She led me completely into my role and then gracefully helped me to perform it. For quite some minutes at a stretch I forgot entirely who I was. I took *him* on, altogether, and surrendered myself to the womanly charm, the totally feminine enchantment of my companion. Her mantle of great age seemed to have fallen from her shoulders like an unwanted cloak—although of course ordinarily I was aware of it; she seemed uncannily to have the power to make me forget her years; she radiated such tenderness and warmth, such sympathy, that I was, for these moments, totally captivated.

As I have said, all went well for the better part of an hour. I glanced at the clock: ten minutes to five. I felt pleased with myself. This had been a good day's work; soon I would have proved myself—for that was, as I understood it, the object of our activities—and I would be allowed to see, at least, her precious little package. Very probably, I thought, I would be allowed to have it altogether, so warm was her feeling for me now.

We fell silent, gathering our wits to play out our finale. She looked away from me; she contemplated the leaping flames in the hearth. The clock ticked very loud just then; bitter wind tore around the corner of the house, tentacles of overgrown shrubbery scratched at the windows. I was content to wait her out—it was, after all, her show. I took a piece of Triphena's Sally Lunn—heavenly!—and nibbled at it in a meditative way. Probably, I thought, I should have to rent a special safe-deposit box.

Suddenly she spoke. "What are you going to do about Mrs. Locke?" she said. She spoke with such intensity that I was quite startled; further, she caught me with a mouth full of cake, so that I needed quickly to choke it down before I could answer. I was aware that my slow and awkward response was a painfully inadequate reply to the urgency of her question.

"Ah—nothing, I think," I said.

"Nothing? But she will ruin us—she will ruin *me*. Are you aware of what she plans to do?"

"She wrote to me—yes—but I think she threatens only. I do not believe that even a Jane Ermina Locke would commit such a slander."

"She would commit it ten times over if she thought she could succeed. You do not know her as I do–she is dangerous. Her hatred of us—of *me*—knows no limits."

I hesitated. What she said was true enough. There is no species on earth so vicious as the literary female. It is a beast capable of the most ferocious behavior even in tranquillity; when it is aroused to anger, its bared fangs and unsheathed claws strike terror into every heart. Every prudent soul flees its wrath; to be ravaged by so bloodthirsty a predator is a nightmare from which one struggles to awake.

"She will not succeed," I said at last. "She knows that a

111

word from me to the right people would prevent her from publishing any of her so-called poems anywhere again. No responsible editor, hearing my side of the story, would print another line by Mrs. Locke if she chooses to continue with her—her novel, is it?"

But even as I spoke I heard the hollow sound of my voice. My response was weak—fatally weak—and we both knew it. There are editors in every city who would delight in my humiliation; my voice can reach only a very few of that pernicious tribe.

"Her filthy fiction—yes!" She spat it out. "She threatens to write three hundred pages—at least—based, she says, on us—but you know what those pages will contain. They will be lies—base, foul lies—she will throw the mud, and it will stick! It always does! Oh—what will we do? How can we silence her?" She wept; her bosom heaved. From somewhere she produced a handkerchief to wipe her eyes.

Really, she presented a deeply touching picture. A man needed a heart of stone to remain unmoved by such a sight. I stood up, I went to her side and bent over her. I took the handkerchief—a useless little scrap of lace-trimmed gauze—and tenderly dried her tears. I murmured soothing phrases—anything that came to mind—I patted her arm, I poured a fresh cup of tea for us both. I drew my chair somewhat closer to hers, I put her cup into her hands. By the time we had swallowed our tea she had recovered a good deal of her composure. Some women have a knack for weeping in a pretty way: They can cry at will with hardly any disfigurement. She was one of these. She smiled at me—at last!—with clear eyes and pale skin.

"I am sorry to burden you with this petty thing," she said. "You are right—she will not dare. But just in case— will you devise a plan to stop her?"

"Ah—yes. Of course."

"Good! Oh, how clever you are! And will you tell me what it is when I see you again?"

"The very next time."

She smiled at me with all her former radiance. As she clasped my hands I heard the clock strike five. It was our signal. She let me go, she nodded dismissal. I was able to leave knowing that her mind was at peace, at least temporarily.

But this happy feeling vanished as I ascended the stairs to my room. Why had I been so concerned for her just now? Why had I experienced so profound a sense of relief when I saw that I had comforted her? I had believed her distress to be genuine. I had forgotten the fact of her role. Had she?

I paused, then, to do something that ordinarily I did not—I stood a step or two above the first landing and looked at Annie Richmond's portrait. Since that first day when I had seen all too clearly what it showed, I had purposely avoided looking at it. Its revelation of its subject was too stark to endure when I had to turn from the canvas to the living flesh. Dissembler that I was, I had my limits.

But I had hardly focused my eyes upon it when I heard the click of the front door latch. It had to be Lenore—there was no one else to come in since Triphena, as far as I could tell, never left the house. I would rather have died than have Lenore see me in my costume. I fled upstairs, where (more skilled each day with practice) I rapidly transformed myself. I folded the black clothes neatly and put them away in the drawer. I looked around the room. Bed, bureau, washstand, table—I was sick of looking at them. They oppressed me; I was in the mood for something more pleasing to the eye. I am, I think, more than ordinarily sensitive to my surroundings. Put me in a sumptuous room and I expand, I thrive, my spirit positively

113

blooms; put me, on the other hand, into a dreary chamber such as this and I wither. And yet I did not want to go back to the parlor, where Mrs. Richmond might still be entrapped in her past; and I could hardly enter the dining room and hang about irritating Triphena, who would be laying the table for dinner and who would most definitely resent my early intrusion.

I decided, therefore, to spend a little time with the portrait. Now that I was properly dressed I did not mind if Lenore came upon me; I would, in fact, welcome her. I was beginning to feel the effects of my continued isolation from the world. Lenore, at least, was sane and steady; whether or not she was friendly to my cause, I knew that her mind was irrevocably *here,* and not wandering back and forth across the years. Furthermore, I longed to ask her—delicately, of course—why she had informed on me.

I went out, shutting my door behind me (what a house of closed doors this was!). I descended to the spot above the landing which gave the best perspective; I contemplated once again that attempt of Hough's to capture in paint and canvas something which no modest eye ought ever to see.

My perceptions of this painting were now, of course, tempered by my knowledge of the nature and personality of the subject. My initial reaction had been to condemn artist, portrait, and Mrs. Richmond herself—most especially Mrs. Richmond, for not having had the decency to burn, or at least to hide away, such a damning exposure. But now, despite the difficult course over which she led me—or perhaps because of it—I was, I realized, much more sympathetic both to her and to Hough's representation. Whether through innocence or perverse vanity (I suspected the former) she had chosen to display it. Those of us who looked at it, therefore, should do so with the greatest possible understanding and kindness of heart.

I sat on the stairs and contemplated it. It seemed to me not quite so revolting as before. He had captured, after all, something of her charm—her feminine charm, as opposed to that other, darker enticement—and perhaps even that quality, repugnant as it was, was merely an aspect of that nasty temper which it had been my misfortune to endure.

I heard the murmur of voices from beyond the closed parlor door—mother and daughter taking tea. I felt lonely just then; I wished that Lenore would come out and talk to me for a while. Our conversations at dinner were entirely superficial, and Mrs. Richmond discouraged any talk at all during our evening readings.

As if in answer to my thought, the parlor door opened just then. Lenore came out. I stood up, preparing to greet her, but before I could say anything she turned on the threshold for a final word to her mother. She raised her voice—I heard every syllable distinct.

"I will see to it. Even now it is almost too late."

She came out into the hall, shutting the door behind her. I hesitated. To speak now was to reveal that I had heard her; on the other hand, if she came upstairs, she would see me and so realize the implication of my silence. She would think that I had been deliberately eavesdropping. I compromised by forcing a little cough. At once she raised her head. Our eyes met. How angry—how very hostile she looked! Really, I did not know whose behavior was more puzzling—hers or her mother's.

"Excuse me," I said. "I did not mean to startle you."

"Didn't you?"

"Positively not. That is the last thing in the world I want to do."

"Then I have read you wrong. I thought that the last thing in the world that you want to do is to go away from us empty-handed."

"You are very harsh."

She walked slowly toward the stairs; she stopped at the first step.

"Are you spying on us now? Why are you standing there—why not come down and have tea? There is no charge."

Ah, I thought, but there is! And I have paid it!

"I have already had mine," I said. "I was just looking once again at your mother's portrait."

She came up, heavily, as if she were very tired.

"It was obvious, to me at least, that you were mightily shocked by it the other day," she said. "Have you changed your opinion?"

"Ah—yes, I have." I smiled at her; she halted on the top step but one. "I think—now—that at least she can be—ah—forgiven for hanging it."

As before, she looked at neither the portrait nor me. She put her hand on the newel post and studied the spread of her fingers. "How generous of you," she said.

"But we must be generous. Certain people must be allowed their—eccentricities. Their misplaced vanities, if you will."

The corners of her mouth drew down in contempt. "Only certain people?"

"Well—everyone, if you insist. But certainly someone like your mother."

"Because of who she is?"

"Because of—what she has been."

I could think of no more delicate way to express my sentiments, but even so her eyes flashed a warning glance at me. She stepped up to the landing, she came past me and

116

continued on to the second floor. I was surprised and a little hurt; in spite of everything I had been sure that she was at least mildly friendly toward me. I had thought that she would welcome, as I did, a chance for a little conversation unchaperoned—undirected by her mother. As I have said, her chief attraction for me at this moment was her unquestioned mental health—her undeniable sanity. I felt that I was beginning ever so slightly to lose my way; she had begun to assume the qualities of a fixed point—a steady North Star—to the wildly swinging needle of my emotions' compass. But on she went, inexorable, leaving me alone on the stair. When she reached the top, she turned to look down at me. For lack of any better appeal, I smiled at her once again.

And now that she was leaving me, her face relaxed. To my surprise, she smiled in return. She seemed about to speak; then, thinking better of it, perhaps, she turned slowly away from me and went on to her room. I heard the door open and close.

Really, I was very sorry to see her go.

14

THE PROBLEM with which Mrs. Richmond had confronted me—the problem of Mrs. Locke—was in fact no small matter. I spent a good deal of time the following day turning it over in my mind; I wanted very much to reassure Mrs. Richmond and ease her fears. (Not incidentally, of course, I wanted to have her version of *l'affaire Locke:* What depths of revengeful spirit must have dwelt within the unprepossessing exterior of that now forgotten poetastress!)

The few known facts in the case were tantalizing in the extreme to anyone with any imagination. Jane Ermina Locke was a prolific versifier who maintained—undoubtedly at her own instigation—a thriving correspondence with the literati. Here I will add a personal observation: If Mrs. Locke had been a man, she might have been a better poet (she could hardly have been a worse one) but she would never have amassed her enormous collection of letters—autographs, if you will—from the prominent literary people of her day. But because she was a member of the weaker sex, those gentlemen, declining to offend her, took the time from their busy lives to answer her communications. She was, it would seem, one of those indomitable lion hunters who, sighting their prey, pursue it over hill and dale—through jungle and desert; through parlor and music room—tracking it to the very door of its lair where, triumphant, they throw out their net and capture it alive.

It must be granted Mrs. Locke that she had an unerring sense of who would be her most likely victim. Hearing of the financial difficulties—no, of the very real and deadly poverty—of the author whose weird croaking bird had so lately thrilled the nation's soul, she organized a public charitable campaign in his behalf. The humiliation which he must have suffered as a result of her solicitations can only be imagined. For a man as proud as he to be forced to endure the attentions of so blatant a climber must have been a more bitter cup than any hemlock.

He declined her "charity." Although all the world knew the truth, he denied that he and his "Muddie"—Mrs. Clemm, mother of his late wife—were starving. Starving! In a country which gave shelter to the flotsam and jetsam of the entire globe! In a country where any man with enough blather and gall could become next thing to a millionaire in the wink of an eye! Mrs. Locke's outrage at the nation's failure to support its greatest genius is perfectly understandable. It is simply her methods which I disdain. She was, apparently, incapable of offering discreet, disinterested aid. For her, the help had to be paid for, publicly acknowledged, by the lion himself.

She enticed him to Lowell with a lecture fee. He came—how could he not? And—money or no—he received a gift beyond price: He met Mrs. Richmond. Instantly Mrs. Locke was forgotten. The world—*his* world—now revolved around

> . . . the thought of the light
> Of the eyes of my Annie.

Naturally Mrs. Locke was furious—what right had this upstart to snatch away the prize?

He removed himself from Mrs. Locke's prying gaze; he came away from Lowell. But she was—do not forget it—a literary female. She determined to have her revenge. She ran to Annie's husband and spat out her mouthful of bile; she wrote to *him*—imagine it!—and told him of her proposed "novel" based on the affair. Nothing came of it; perhaps her courage failed, or perhaps—would I soon discover it?—Annie's husband bought her off. At any rate, it must have been a turbulent time for all concerned. I needed all my cunning to devise a satisfactory answer to Mrs. Richmond's urgent plea.

The next afternoon I dressed with especial care. I knew that he, shabby though he was, was always meticulously neat and clean; it must have been his way of saying to the world: "You can never defeat me as long as my coat is brushed, my boots polished." My heart beat with a not unpleasant excitement as I prepared myself. I realized that I had come to look forward to this daily confrontation—this daily test to which she put me.

I descended precisely on the hour. She smiled at me, she welcomed me in. Her hand was steady as she gave me my cup; her eyes were clear and calm as they met mine. I was relieved; I had feared to find her distraught, and I wanted a little time to ease into my role before our serious business began.

We spoke of ciphers for a while, and then she asked me to describe for her the actions of Maelzel's chess player. That was no task at all for me, prepared as I was. I went on unhesitatingly for quite fifteen minutes before she stopped me with a wave of her hand. Ah, I thought, now we come to it. I tensed, ready to explain to her the course of action which I had determined to follow regarding Mrs. Locke's alarming threats.

But no—she handed me the volume, already marked, and bade me read aloud. I was a little disappointed; I had been so very sure that what I had planned to say would please her. Still, I had no choice, and so for the next half hour I read: "Annabel Lee," "The Raven," "The City in the Sea," "A Dream Within a Dream."

I glanced at her now and then as I spoke some particularly felicitous, sensuous line. She sat with her eyes shut, a faint smile upon her lips. I heard my voice going on and on; I wondered if she were aware, as I was, of the deep resonance of its timbre, the echo of the Southern slur which made the words I read seem all the more affecting. (I admit it: The New England twang can deal adequately—no more—with prose; it massacres fine poetry.)

At last I finished. I closed the book, I placed it gently on the table. She did not move; I wondered if perhaps—she was after all very old—if perhaps she had gone to sleep.

I cleared my throat. At the first sound her eyes flew open. To my great consternation her face was suddenly very angry. Why? What had I done wrong?

"Do not clear your throat in that irritating way," she said.

"I beg your pardon."

"Men of genius do not clear their throats."

"Never?"

"Never. It is a sign of hesitation. It is almost an apology for existing. Men of genius know that they do not have to apologize for anything."

I let it pass; I would not argue with her.

"You think me petty to dwell upon such a small point. But I want everything to be—perfect. No detail can be overlooked."

"I understand."

"I wonder if you do? It is a matter of attitude, you see. Not only must you put on certain clothing, you must put on an attitude as well. A way of thinking—a way of looking at things. All the study in the world will not suffice if you do not have that."

"Yes."

She made a small sound of irritation. "Do not always be so quick to agree with me! Have opinions of your own— and defend them! Who am I, after all? Who is anyone, compared to you? We are only common folk, but you— you are one man in a generation—in a century! You must behave as if you believe that. You must develop a certain arrogance. People expect it of you."

I could think of no reply that would not anger her more. Despite what she said, I was sure that she wanted no real disagreement from me. Were I truly to become what she said she wanted, I would be banished at once. No. She wanted the appearance of difficulty only, not the thing itself. I cast swiftly about for some way to turn the conversation to our problem of the previous day, but she spoke before I could find the words.

"I have told Triphena to put paper and pen in your room. I would like to have you work a little—to write something for me. It has been a long time since you have produced anything. You are better now—you have had a

123

good rest, nourishing food, you are much stronger than you were before. Mr. Willis has assured me that he will welcome anything you send to him."

Once again she had outwitted me; once again I was checkmated by that cunning of the mad which puts the sane at such a disadvantage. Write something! And what, pray, might it be, dear lady? Would you have me—*me*— toss off a little macabre made to order? A hymn to Beauty, perhaps, embellished with my special style? Or should I resurrect Dupin?

I uttered the beginnings of a protest, but even as she held up her hand to silence me she smiled upon me once again.

"You can do it. I have complete faith that you can."

"You are mistaken. I cannot."

"Try."

" 'Try' be damned—excuse me." Had I so far forgotten myself that I swore in front of a lady? "What you ask is impossible." It was an inadequate reply, although I tried to put a little hauteur in my tone.

Her eyes gleamed at me, encouraging me. "You will do it. I know you will."

"You are deluding yourself—"

"No! Do not say that!" Her tone was angry but her eyes, her lips, smiled at me. "I know what I ask. You must have faith in yourself. You must believe in what you can do."

"It is not a question of belief—"

"But it is! It is! You must gear yourself up to it—wind up your brain to a high pitch of intensity! Then you will see— you will do it!"

She had herself become so intense during this exhortation that she leaned forward in her chair as if she were poised to spring at me. Her face was alight with hope, with faith—in me!—her voice trembled with the urgency of her thought. For a moment she almost succeeded in transmitting her vision to me. I was aware of a curious warm feeling—a glow—spreading inside me, a hot bright current energizing my brain—

"One more thing." She relaxed; her voice was matter-of-fact again, all business. "As good as your appearance is, it is not yet perfect." She considered me; dumbly I awaited her pronouncement. Finally she said, "You must be careful with your razor. You are no good at all without a moustache."

15

Mrs. Richmond did not come down to dinner that night, but her spirit was very much there with us. We were, Lenore and I, acutely aware of the vacant place at the head of the table, and as we consumed our lamb chops and baked potatoes we kept our conversation as light, as trivial as it would have been had Mrs. Richmond herself sat there. Of course Triphena, too, was a preventative to more than casual discourse. She served with practiced efficiency, which meant that we were at every moment aware of her presence just beyond the door if not actually at table.

As had become our custom after dinner we took our coffee into the parlor. She shut the door—a curiously intimate gesture signaling our certain privacy. After poking up the fire and throwing on another log, she went to stand by the table, her fingers resting on the book of poems from which I had read to her mother that afternoon. For one dreadful moment I thought that she was going to ask me to read again as was our evening practice with Mrs. Richmond. But she came away; she settled herself in her usual place on the sofa, while I took my chair by the fire. She looked unusually attractive as she sat with her arm outstretched along the curved back; I wondered that I had not noticed her appearance earlier at dinner. I did not want to stare too boldly at her, and yet I was intrigued—what had she done to herself? Her face reflected somewhat more color than usual. Was it the firelight, or had she—at last!—applied some artificial aid to Nature? And if she had, was it for my benefit? I cast my careful eye over her figure. Cosmetics or no, she did not seem sufficiently motivated to please me to encase herself in a corset.

I was glad of this time alone with her; as I have said, I was beginning to feel uncomfortably off balance, and she was at least sane, if not always congenial. Then, too, I had my question that I wanted to put to her. Since it was rather rude, I knew that I would have to prepare the way for it very carefully. I was glad that we had the evening before us, since possibly I would need all that time. I did not want to alarm her, to anger her. I simply wanted to ask her to play fair.

"So!" I said, as brightly as I could. "And did you have a pleasant day today? It is very strange, but I still do not know what it is that you do with your time."

"I have my own affairs."

"Obviously." I smiled at her; I paused to allow her to enlighten me. She chose not to do so; instead, after sipping her coffee for a moment or two, she went uncomfortably straight to the point—*my* point.

"Are you succeeding?" she said.

Useless to ask at what; better to play her way and so more easily, perhaps, get to my own concern.

"I don't know. It is very difficult."

"Most things are."

"Yes. But then it is a matter simply of deciding whether the game is worth the candle."

"And this one is?"

"Certainly. I am still here, am I not?"

She granted me my point; I derived a certain grim satisfaction from the knowledge that she was not in fact aware of just how difficult the game had proved to be. I contemplated telling her. What would she say about her mother's behavior? Would she move to have her certified, put away, shut up in the McLean Asylum? But such an event would have no advantage for me—none. As far as I was concerned—at least at this moment—Lenore needed to know nothing about my daily charades.

The fact of my superior knowledge emboldened me, then, to move far more swiftly than I had planned to my own question for her.

"The last time we were in this room alone," I said, "I persuaded you so successfully of the worth of my cause that you consented to help me. I think I understand why you did not simply give me what I sought—there is, after all, a certain honor to be maintained by both of us. But I cannot understand at all why you then deliberately betrayed me before I had had even a sporting chance to succeed."

"Betrayed you?" Her face assumed a baffled expression. "If I betrayed anyone—and why do you use so strong a word?—surely it was not you."

"I had not been here ten minutes alone when she discovered me. Someone must have alerted her."

She seemed truly mystified. "So that was it! I thought that you simply couldn't find the spring."

"I could not—that is true. But I would have—I am sure I

would have—if I had been given time. She came in not moments after you went out."

"And so you think—oh, but that's ridiculous!" She actually laughed. "You ascribe to me the qualities of a Machiavelli. I assure you I am not nearly so devious—I haven't the slightest propensity to intrigue."

I did not believe a word of it, but I allowed some of the puzzlement of her expression to pass into my own.

"But if you did not tell her—alert her—then who did? Triphena knew nothing—"

"No. It was not Triphena, you can be sure of that. She always goes to bed directly after she clears dinner and she sleeps very soundly. No—" She thought for a moment. "Why do you think that anyone told her at all?"

"Because, dear lady, she came down. She found me out. I felt like a thief in the night. It was most embarrassing, I assure you."

"Yes. It must have been." To her credit she remained perfectly sober; she had at least the sensitivity not to smile at the thought of my predicament. "But I think you have overlooked something perfectly obvious," she continued. "She came down—yes. She had been alerted. But not necessarily by anyone else. Do you see? Something in her own mind could have warned her. I am not a believer in psychic phenomena, but I do think that somehow some warning might have penetrated to her sleeping brain. Somehow she knew that her treasure was being disturbed—"

"Of course the possibility of this—ah—psychic phenomenon did not occur to you when you agreed to show me the panel."

"Of course not. How could it? Nothing like it—nothing like *you*—has ever happened before." A faint smile—how like her mother's!—curved her lips.

"All those others—?"

130

Her smile remained, and yet I felt a tremor of apprehension, for her friendliness, her amusement with me, had suddenly disappeared. Her smile remained, yes, but it was now an unpleasant thing, vaguely contemptuous. "Oh—they were nothing compared to you. Some of them were quite persistent, of course. Once Triphena even had to threaten to go to the neighbors' and use their telephone to call the police. The man simply refused to leave. He thought we were quite an easy mark."

I imagined the scene: the desperate treasure-hunter (how like myself!) in hot pursuit of his goal, the intransigent women stoutly rebuffing him—poor fellow! My heart bled for him a little—but not too much, of course, since his failure predicated my success. What, I wondered, had happened to him? How had he managed to live on without the prize?

As if she read my thoughts she said, still smiling, "We managed to get rid of him, finally, without calling for help."

"I am sure you did," I said. "You are, as I recall, most resourceful and efficient at repelling intruders. By the time I appeared you'd certainly had enough practice. Were they all as determined as I?"

"Of course not. Some of them—most of them—never even got through the door. Ingram was different, of course. He applied by letter, and as I have told you, my mother was sufficiently impressed with his credentials to copy out certain passages for him. But most of them we discouraged as they stood on the porch. And of course not one of them had your—ah—ingenuity."

"Not to mention my charm."

She laughed outright, then, as I had intended her to do. I did not like her curious smile! I felt uncomfortably deflated. I had not expected her to deny my accusation—

131

or at least not with such a fantastic tale—but now, having received that denial, I was prepared to grant it to her and move on to more rewarding topics. She had after all encouraged me just now with her recital of the failure of all those other devotees.

But once again she was quicker than I. "Do you know my mother's real name?" she said.

"Her—her maiden name, do you mean?"

"No. Her original given name."

"It is not 'Annie?' But why then did he immortalize—"

"He called her that. Her name was Nancy. For reasons which we will probably now never know, he preferred the other. She never again answered to her own—my father, everyone, had to address her as 'Annie.' She changed it legally, in court, after my father died."

Interesting! "A rose by any other name—" I smiled at her. She had seemed to offer this revelation as a consolation prize. It was hardly that, of course, but I appreciated her intent.

You may wonder, when I was sitting not ten feet away from the bookcase, why I did not simply repeat my request to her and, when again she had opened the panel, take what lay within.

I can only reply that, having failed that chance—for whatever reason—I felt that it would be a betrayal of Mrs. Richmond that evening to snatch the prize towards which, daily, I worked with her. I could, at that moment, have asked Lenore to open the panel again; I could have read the letters, perhaps even escaped with them. But I did not. Call me a fool if you will. To me it was, now, a matter of my honor. I had passed by the easier route; I was embarked now on the more difficult path, and on that rocky way I would succeed or fail. I was not now in a position morally to do anything else.

132

And so I let the moment pass and once again I turned the conversation to Lenore's life. This time she was more willing to respond; perhaps because I had amused her? Or because she felt sorry for me?

She told me then—really for the first time—something about herself. I confess that I was astonished at what I heard, although certainly I knew well enough that she was no ordinary female. But this! I could not understand. It seemed so intolerably dreary.

"Think what it must be for them." she said. "I am there only a few hours a day."

"But—you might catch a disease! They are fearfully dirty."

"They are poor. Cleanliness is expensive."

"How do you communicate with them? Most of them can't speak a word that one can understand."

"I get along. I'm quite comfortable in French, of course, and I've picked up a surprising amount of Polish. Now the Greeks have begun to come, and I shall have to learn that."

"Amazing." Truly, I could hardly comprehend it. "But why do you paint them? Why not paint landscape—the river valley here must afford a wealth of scenic views."

"I am not interested in scenic views, or at least not that kind. I am interested in faces. In faces—as I see them."

"Why not paint your friends then?"

She hesitated a moment before she answered. Then: "I have no friends."

"Oh, but surely—" I had never heard such an admission from anyone.

"No. Or at least—none in my own—what might have been my own circle. As you may have noticed, we have no callers here. You were the first in a long time. We hardly ever go out socially. We hardly even go to church. Most of my mother's contemporaries are gone, and I—" She

133

paused; painfully she continued. "I went to the Seminary at Mount Holyoke. I had a few friends there. When I came home again I knew what I wanted to do—how I wanted to spend my time. My mother insisted that I apply myself to finding a husband. But no one—no one suitable—ever appeared. And so after a time I began my lessons with Alfred Byam—he had instructed Hough also—and after he died, I proceeded alone."

"And all these years you have painted—them?"

"No. Only for the last three or four. As you say, we are surrounded here by picturesque views. I painted them—very badly. Often, too, in the summer I went to Gloucester and Nahant and painted seascapes. Badly also. Even though I was glad to be working, it was not right somehow—I was searching for something—scenes, landscapes, subjects—that I could not find in nature."

"And these people are what you sought?"

"Partly."

"Why? What do you see in them?"

"I don't know. A kind of energy—a kind of life, I suppose."

"Life! Most of them look half dead to me."

"No—not if you look closely. They have a wonderful directness. They are simple people, they lack the layers of artifice and sophistication behind which many people hide—people of my circle, as you might say, or of yours even more. I cannot explain it well—they hold a fascination for me which I try to capture on canvas. The results are . . . not the ordinary thing, but that is unimportant."

"You work—among them? Do you pay them?"

"I have a room in a tenement, and I work here also. And I do pay them, yes—fifty cents an hour for the hard labor of sitting for me. To them it is great wealth, of course."

"You must have a thousand canvases if you have been doing this for three or four years."

"No. Many times I simply talk with them."

"Do you pay them for that, too?"

It was a cruel thrust, but I could not resist it. I was certain that she had lied to me in the matter of my discovery; and I was certain, too, that her talk of her association with the immigrants was the most disgusting thing that I had heard in a long time. She was, in her own way, as eccentric as her mother. I was sorry to hear it—deeply disappointed in her.

She did not reply; and after a moment, in a voice as kind as I could make it—my apology, which she understood—I said, "I should very much like to see your work. Have you had an exhibition?"

"Not yet. One cannot have an exhibition here, for real success one must go to Boston or New York, and I find it more difficult each year to get away. I do not know anyone—"

"You know me."

She stared at me with sudden, sharp attention.

"Do you forget that I am a member of the Boston Art Club? I know every dealer in the city and a good many in New York. If you think that you are ready—"

"Oh, I am. But—"

"'But' nothing! Can you show me what you have done? Where do you keep your canvases?"

"Here—there is a room in back, only the kitchen stairs lead to it, I cleared it and made it into a studio when I began—"

She had half risen from her seat. She seemed bemused, as if she were not sure of the sincerity of my interest. I stood up, I smiled at her, I held out my hand to her in a gesture of encouragement. I understood her feelings completely. Everyone is shy about showing his work; only repeated acclaim gives confidence. At last she rose; she led me out through the back hall to the kitchen, where Tri-

135

phena was just finishing the dishes; she led me to the stairway to her workroom.

You will remember that on my first night with the Richmonds I spoke kindly to Lenore in an attempt to show that I appreciated her help to me. This instinct to placate those who help us now worked, I saw, very strongly in her. Her attitude toward me had changed completely from civil antagonism to overt appeasement. As we climbed the narrow dim stairs, our way lit by a lamp which she had picked up in the kitchen, she murmured phrases of self-deprecation, of gratitude for my interest—schoolgirlish phrases, ingenue words which sounded odd coming from one ordinarily so self-contained.

I was delighted to hear them. As I have explained, I had determined to win by direct combat with Mrs. Richmond rather than by subterfuge with her daughter. But I could not ignore altogether the possibility that I might fail with the mother and so be forced, in the end, to turn once again for help to Lenore. If I could in the meantime find a way to put her in my debt, so much the better when the time arrived (as I hoped it would not) to force my claim.

As near as I could make it out, Lenore's studio was situated on the river side of the house on the third floor, adjacent to the attic. I could not tell if there was a connecting door because the dividing wall was hidden by a huge cabinet containing, I supposed, her paints and canvas. As we entered she put the lamp on a littered table in the center of the room. I saw an easel upon which rested a half-finished portrait; a worn divan by the window; a bookcase. Ranged around the walls were perhaps a dozen canvases.

I could not have said what I expected to find: badly done imitations of the Academicians, say, or, despite her dismissal of the subject, undigested chunks of landscape after the Hudson River School. Certainly I did not expect what in fact I saw: Never, save in certain European museums, had I seen paintings like these. Had she seen them too? Or were these—these grotesqueries!—entirely the product of her own mind, which until this moment had impressed me as solidly, dependably sane?

She did not look at me as I examined them. She stood by the table, her eyes downcast, her attitude that of the most extreme shyness. I had already decided as we climbed the stairs that if I did not like her work, I would tell her so at once; but I had hoped that that opinion would not be necessary. I had resolved to make every allowance for her inexperience, her possible lack of talent, lack of training—even for her unfortunate choice of subjects. Every benefit of every doubt would be hers, I thought. Surely I would be able to think of someone—some small dealer—who would take on a few of her better efforts, no matter how amateurish.

But these! Whatever else they were, they were not the work of a Sunday painter, a maiden lady who decorates canvas in her spare time. Bold, startling—the product of a firm, sure hand—but what of the brain that conceived them? I felt that I looked here on evidence of a distorted vision—a spiritual, not a physical vision—warped and thwarted beyond the wildest nightmares of ordinary folk.

Can I convey them in words? I must try.

The first canvas nearest the door was one of the largest in the room, perhaps three feet by four. It was—after all!—a landscape, but the scenery was of the Devil's domain. Diagonally across the canvas flowed a river—a foaming, tumultuous torrent rushing toward some unseen destination. The water was blood red. In its current bobbed writhing, drowning creatures whose contorted faces screamed silently for rescue. In the background loomed the black bulks of factory buildings whose lighted windows

137

mirrored the Hellish color of the river; their tall smoke-stacks blasted fire, their facades crawled with monstrous insects—no, not insects. People—nearly human!—hideous, winged, many-legged creatures with faces such as one saw in any mill yard, who, trying to escape, fell one by one into the boiling crimson tide below. Along the banks of the river stood phalanxes of armored—what? cockroaches?—who wielded pikestaves to thrust back into the water any wretch who tried to crawl ashore. Overhead arched a swirling purple sky mottled with black clouds; jagged lightning ripped its edge at the horizon.

I glanced at her. I realized that I was trembling. She met my gaze with a look half-pleading, half-defiant. Neither of us spoke. I moved on.

The next canvas was smaller. It was at first glance a rendering of a verdant Eden. But of course it was not that at all. Monstrous vegetation never seen on this earth formed a backdrop for a group of dancing figures, totally unclothed, their flesh raw with running sores covering their deformities—a hunched back, a withered leg, a misshapen skull. From the background—the jungle—peered other creatures. Or were these the plants themselves, the faces their blossoming flowers? And animals and birds, too, danced in the scene. I saw a lion, a peacock, a prancing unicorn, an owl—and, looking closer, I saw that they did more than dance. They coupled, they grappled with the naked figures—yes, and just there, in the corner, in a curious many-turreted castle whose wall was torn away, revealing the interior—there lay a female giving birth to the results of that coupling. A creature emerged—crawled!—from her womb, furred and feathered both and yet bearing the face of a human child—

I turned away. I could not bear what I saw. It was too powerful, it spoke to something deep in my soul—something I had not known existed. I had never seen anything like this—no, not even abroad! She had shown me a maddened view of a species irrevocably lost to the Devil. Did I now dare show it to the world? For, despite my disgust, I was something of a connoisseur after all; I knew good work when I saw it. We may disagree with the artist's vision; we cannot argue his ability. How in Heaven's name had she come by this—this unearthly genius? Was she, after all, his child? And had his imaginative powers been transmitted to her to find expression in a different medium?

Finally, regaining some control over my badly shaken sensibilities, I was able to look at her.

"I must beg your pardon," she said then, quickly. "I did not expect a visitor to this room—no one ever comes. Had I known that you were to inspect my work, I would have put away certain items. Here—come over to this wall." She put out her hand, she led me across the room. "Have a look at some of these," she said. "They are not quite so— out of the ordinary."

I had flinched at the sensation of her touch, but now, as we gazed together at these other examples of her work, I relaxed and let my hand rest easy in hers. What on earth was she? What, really, went on in that maidenly heart, that sharp brain? My mind wandered for a moment to a forbidden place. I could not help myself. All men think so; it is part of our nature to speculate on the amorous potential of a woman—any woman—who has in some way aroused our curiosity. One speculates, one ponders the difficulties—there are always difficulties—one attempts to sample the goods. It is the way of the world: women, horses, *objets d'art*, railroad securities, precious papers—we take, we buy as we can. Whatever else her painting showed, I thought, it was unquestionably the product of a passionate nature. I longed now, just for a moment, to test that nature—to see for myself how deep, how warm her passion ran.

Somehow she must have sensed my thoughts (as her mother, so she claimed, had sensed my covetous actions?). She withdrew her hand from mine; she stepped away from me a bit.

"Here," she said. "These are taken—as you see—from some of his tales. Of course it is always a question of whether paint and canvas can duplicate the powers of the imagination. Very often they cannot. And yet I think that these are not too bad."

I responded to her hint and murmured an appreciative comment or two. I was glad to be able to do it. What I saw now was not nearly so overwhelming as those others. These showed a more conventional—and therefore more comfortable—horror. The familiar scenes met my eye: the rotting, putrescent mass which once was M. Valdemar, the wretched prisoner watching the descent of the razor-edged pendulum, the death agonies of Roderick and Madeline Usher.

I was positively glad to see them. Dear old friends!

"And here," she said, leading me along, "here is a little conceit. This would never be put for sale, of course."

Grant her her good sense on one point, at least, I thought. *What* was she thinking of? For here, all gathered together on the same small canvas, was himself, black-clothed (even as I!), black bird on his shoulder, volume open in hand, and here, too, was Mrs. Richmond, very young, very beautiful—and with them was Lenore! The two lovers, whose pose indicated their roles, were situated in a garden—an ordinary garden—and they were pictured in miniature duplicate on a tiny canvas on an easel; they were in fact painted posing for a visible portrait. And the artist—glaring anachronism!—was Lenore.

140

Had I not seen all those other revelations, I would have thought this last canvas a charming attempt, perhaps, to please her mother. As it was I did not know what to think. A personality which had produced those other landscapes was hardly to be trusted even when it gave forth the most ordinary-looking effort. I looked closer. Yes! I was positive—yes, certainly! What had seemed to be a conventional Gothic ruin in the background of misty trees was in fact a human figure, lurking, spying—

She was not capable, it seemed, of producing a straightforward representation. Everything, for her, had peculiar hidden meanings which she felt compelled to portray.

I pondered my dilemma. I had offered to help her to get a viewing from a dealer. Had I been less eager to put her in my debt, I would have waited until I had seen her work. But I had rushed ahead, committing myself, never dreaming what lay waiting for my observation. Now, somehow, I had to follow through. I could not refuse now to help her and so possibly make an enemy where I had hoped to secure a friend.

On the other hand, what dealer would risk displaying these works? Technical ability, vivid imagination, haunting visions—yes, all very well, but what of the man's reputation? Could I convince someone? Who?

She understood. "Never mind," she said. "You see the difficulty. I work as I will, but my work is not calculated to win easy approval."

In the harsh glare of the kerosene lamp she smiled at me. My heart suddenly warmed to her. Poor girl! What, after all, was her life? A few canvases, a tenuous contact with the lowliest class of society, an aging and indifferent parent? I must try, I thought, to bring some happiness to her while I accomplish my own mission. The thought gave me a quite unaccustomed sensation of disinterested bene-

141

volence. And besides—these paintings deserved to be seen! I would stake my reputation on them!

"Bother the difficulty," I said. "I have never seen anything like these in my life. You must be exhibited—you will make a sensation!"

An expression of relief—of touching gratitude—suffused her face.

"Where?" she said.

In that instant a name occurred to me. Yes! "Tomorrow!" I said. "I know just the man. We will pack them up and send them off. This one—the Ushers—and the Pit—and—ah—" I turned again to the weird landscapes, I scanned the several which I had forborne to examine closely. I did not want to look at them; they were like the others. They would—I was sure—give me nightmares for weeks to come. "The—ah—smaller one, the dancers—yes, that will give him a fair idea of your style. But not tomorrow. Make it the day after. I will write to him tomorrow. Then he will be sure to have the letter before they arrive."

She smiled at me. "You are really very kind."

"Nonsense! You and your mother both have been so kind to me that if I can in any way return your generosity—"

Her smile faded at the mention of Mrs. Richmond. "You had better not mention this to her."

"Oh? Will she not like it?"

"She will be angry, I think. At any rate, she will think we are conspiring against her. And that will do you no good."

"I don't understand. Does she so very much disapprove?"

"Yes."

"What does she say?"

She hesitated; she shook her head.

"You know that any confidence is safe with me," I said.

142

Finally, very low, "She says that I am wasting my time. She says that I have no talent."

"I would respectfully disagree with her."

"She would remind you that she is an authority on the subject—that she was an early patron of Henry Hough."

"Whom now she describes as second-rate."

"Remember what he did to her."

"Is that the reason?"

"Oh yes. She used to rave about him. He was her eternal topic—how I hated to hear the man's name!"

"But she will not take you up as she took him—and you her own daughter?"

"Ah—" Her mouth twisted into a bitter grimace. "Serious work is not suitable for her daughter. We are ladies of some social standing here, remember—or we were, once. She would not mind if I painted little water colors of the river—as you yourself suggested—or flowers on velvet or some such nonsense. But, by trying to do something seriously—something very much my own—I assert myself too much. She knows I find a kind of freedom in it, and she cannot understand. And because she cannot understand, she resents it."

"And still you go to them? Still you work?"

"We had it out last year. I told her that if she tried to prevent me, I would simply leave her and go and live in the tenement."

"She does want you to stay, then? Even on your terms?"

"She does not want a scandal. To her—to people here—it would be a scandal if I were to move away from home—not to go to Boston or New York or Paris, mind you, although that would be bad enough, but to move down there—to a tenement on Cabot Street. So we have arrived at our equilibrium—I do as I will, but I stay here with her and preserve appearances."

143

And preserve also, no doubt, your place in her last will and testament, I thought. I did not for a moment blame her. Very few of us are foolhardy enough to turn away from what was in this case undoubtedly a sizable inheritance.

"Forgive me—do you have an income of your own?" A rude question, but I very much wanted to know the answer.

"She gives me an allowance."

"Enough to—to pay your models?"

"No. Not enough—not always."

I saw that she wanted to continue, that she took comfort from my friendly interest, but that she needed a little time. I made no reply; I waited.

"Sometimes I—I take money from her. Not much—just enough to pay them, or buy new paint and canvas."

"She never notices?"

"She never mentions it. If she does notice, I am sure that she regards it as merely part of the price she must pay to retain her—our—reputations. That is the important thing to her. No doubt she thinks that it is enough for me to know that when she dies I will be independent."

Her voice had taken on an edge of bitterness—and, worse, of real hatred—that chilled my heart with something very like fear. It seemed so—unnatural!—for a daughter to speak so of her mother! Was this the same daughter who, on first meeting me, had so valiantly defended her mother's fortress? Who had, upon showing me the lock-spring panel, warned me against breaking the old woman's heart?

Depend upon it: The slave will always turn against the master if given the chance. I had broken through the veneer of conventional devotion of child for parent; I had been given a glimpse of the festering resentment, the very

144

real rebellion simmering just there under the calm exterior of their lives.

Do you see? We were both her supplicants, Lenore and I. The knowledge of that fact was another arrow in my quiver—and this new shaft bore a poisoned tip.

16

THE NEXT morning I wrote a few lines to the dealer whom I had mentioned to Lenore and gave the note to her to post. When she had gone—with a reassuring press of my hands in farewell—I settled myself at my writing table and prepared to deal with Mrs. Richmond's latest command.

I arranged the sheets of paper neatly in front of me. I put the inkwell conveniently to hand. I picked up the pen. My mind was empty. I could not think of three words to string together. The immaculate pale blue surface seemed to defy me to blemish it with even a single letter. Many of his stories, of course, were quite short—not more than half a dozen pages. It had seemed to me, contemplating my task, that I should be able to scratch out at least an equal amount. Several little plots—trifling things—had flitted in and out of my brain previous to the time when I sat myself at the table and took up the pen. Now, faced with the actual task of putting words on paper, I was paralyzed.

A title, I thought; if I can get a title, I can go on from there. I concentrated. Nothing came. Single words—"cask," "death," "coffin," "grave"—raced through my mind but refused to stay long enough to form themselves into a coherent phrase. Lenore's painting of the river—of the blood-red river—rose up to my vision. A story perhaps about that weird world? No—no. Mrs. Richmond must not know that I had seen Lenore's work. Lenore had warned me. I remembered her words. I put down the pen; I rested my head in my hands. I was conscious of an unpleasant weakness overtaking my body. My heart pounded, my stomach seemed ready to disgorge its contents. My fingers touched my unshaven upper lip—only one day's growth, and already devilishly annoying! I did not want a moustache; I did not want that disgusting shadow to blight my countenance. I actually went so far as to get up from my chair (with difficulty, because of my weakness) and go to the bureau where lay the razor. I had as usual shaved my face and chin; now, I thought, I will finish the job. She had no right to demand of me so irritating a task. I stared at myself in the mirror. The growth extended across my upper lip like a stain. Ugly—disfiguring!

I picked up the pot of shaving cream. I watched myself. After a time—I do not know how long—I put it down. My hand hurt, so tightly had I held it. Persevere, I thought. You will win in the end. Play it out.

I returned to my table—my seat of torment, as it now seemed. At last a title had occurred to me. I wrote it down, and then, slowly, hesitantly, I began to write the story.

Anyone who has ever tried to compose anything, no matter how trivial, will understand when I say that four or five hours at such work will leave one exhausted. Drawing out a story from one's mind as the spider draws the web from her body—spinning a tale—is the hardest work in the world. I realized when I had done that it was long past lunch time. No matter—I was not hungry. I stacked the sheets—ten in all—which I had written (and laboriously rewritten into a fair copy) and threw myself down on my bed. At once I was asleep. Fortunately some inner alarm—or was it a tap on my door?—awoke me in time to put on my costume and go downstairs to Mrs. Richmond.

I was of course very anxious about our meeting this day. It was not possible that she would find my little tale in any way comparable to one of his. Would the discovery that I was, after all, only myself disturb her so that she would tire of the whole business? And, tiring of it, would she then expel me empty-handed? Would the suspension of disbelief which she so assiduously cultivated in her unpredictable brain finally be unable to function, faced with the inescapable proof that she dealt, not with *him*, but with an imposter? With perspiration uncontrolled, with fast beating heart and trembling knees, I entered the parlor.

She acknowledged my presence; she looked at the manuscript which I held carefully in two hands like an offering.

"What do you have there?" she said.

"The little composition for which you asked."

She held out her hand; I gave it to her. She flipped through the sheets without reading so much as a word. I doubt that she even read the title.

"Why have you given it to me like this?" she said.

I did not understand.

"Why is it not properly prepared?" she said. Her voice had taken on an unpleasant tone.

I shook my head. "I'm sorry. I don't know what you mean."

She held the manuscript tightly in her left hand, wrinkling the pages which I had produced with such difficulty. I could not refrain from uttering a small cry of protest at her disregard for all my work.

"Please—don't."

"Don't *what?*" With a vicious little twist of her mouth she threw down the sheets of close-written paper. They scattered on the floor in front of her. At once I was on my hands and knees gathering them up. I bit my lips to stop myself from berating her. When I had them all I got to my feet with as much dignity as I could summon and then I seated myself at the table to put the pages in order again. She waited in silence until I had finished. I looked at her then, but I said nothing; I was, in truth, close to tears at her brutal reception of my work. Had I been alone, I would undoubtedly have wept; as it was, I controlled myself and raged silently against her.

At last she said, "Forgive me. I should not have done that. It is only—well. Never mind. You could not have known. But I had so longed to see once again that neat little scroll. Did you not know that he always pasted his pages together into one long sheet, and then rolled it and tied it?"

I shook my head, not yet trusting myself to speak.

"Well, he did. And I have sat here today for the longest time, anticipating the *feel* of it—the fat, solid weight of it in my hands. To prepare his manuscripts so was a private eccentricity of his. I should have told you, but that would have spoiled the pleasure of it. I took the chance that somehow you would know."

Her words soothed me somewhat. I was able to smile at her, and then, finally, to speak. "I will paste it as you say and give it to you tomorrow."

"No—no. Never mind. If I have to tell you it is no good.

150

And, after all, the main thing was to give you the experience of composition. Did you enjoy it?"

"No."

She smiled faintly. "It is a humbling experience, is it not? I tried it once myself. I gave up after three pages. But to do it—and to know that one has done it well—ah, *that* must be a satisfaction! That must give one a feeling of—of worth, of power, of—*being*—do you see? He used to cry so often. He would sit at my feet and sob into my lap. For her—for Virginia—sometimes. Otherwise for himself. And I would try to reassure him by saying what I have said just now to you. I used to tell him over and over again that he had been blessed, that he had been given a gift denied the rest of us, that because of his God-given power he was a kind of God himself—"

I held my breath. I was conscious of my immobile body; I willed myself to stay so. Go on, I thought, go on, go on— ah, what could you not tell me!

She had drifted back into her memories, leaving me alone. She sat silent; she looked beyond me at nothing. I was content to wait her out; I would not have spoken for the world. I stared at her, imploring her not to forget me. Take me with you, I begged. Let me have a little of him, too! She blinked; her gaze shifted to me. She seemed about to speak.

I can hardly bear to remember what happened next. I can still feel the shock of it: my nerves unstrung by the tension of the last days—the last hour; my body weakened by the strain on my nerves; my entire system made more vulnerable to the slightest irritant, to a single particle of dust, a single cold current of air— I sneezed.

In that quiet room it was an explosion. She started violently; her hand flew to her heart; her eyes saw me then unquestionably! At once she recovered herself. She gave

151

me her handkerchief, and then, as I helplessly blew my nose, she stood up and went to the sideboard, where she made a small clatter with glass and decanter.

"You must take care of yourself," she said. "Triphena told me you had no lunch today."

"No. I was . . . busy."

"Yes. Well . . . take this." She returned to me with a snifter half full of amber liquid. "And mind you don't miss dinner."

I am not ordinarily a drinking man. During my stay with the Richmonds I had not minded the absence of alcohol. But now that small glass seemed to me to hold the most desirable liquid in the world. I sipped it gratefully; really, it was just what I needed. It flowed easily down my throat; its warmth spread through my body. I sipped some more; I finished it in three large gulps. She returned to her seat. She watched me, smiling at me; I basked in the glow of her approbation.

"There," she said at last. "That's better. Tell me, have your headaches improved? I mean, have they gone away?"

I felt more at ease than at any time since I arrived—when? Ten days ago? It might have been a month—a year. My body was utterly relaxed; my mind floated out on a cloud of well-being. I assured her that my headaches hardly ever troubled me.

"And you have had no fever?"

I assured her that I had not.

"You are a strong man. With proper care there is no reason why you should not live a long time. You feel better; I can see that you do."

I agreed with her. I felt, in fact, positively euphoric.

She leaned toward me; she held out her hand.

"Come here," she said. "Pull your chair in close to mine. No—wait." She rose and took my glass and went again to the sideboard. She came back a moment later with more brandy. I took it; hardly aware of what I did, I swallowed half of it. I felt a drop trickling down my chin. I wiped it with her handkerchief.

"Now. Come close." She sat again; I obeyed her. She took my hand in hers. Her luminous eyes looked into mine. I saw nothing else; I was conscious of nothing but those eyes, the sensation of her touch. When she spoke, her voice plucked the lute strings of my soul.

"You are always in my heart," she said. "Never fear that I will desert you."

Somehow I managed to murmur a reply. My lips felt numb; I could hardly form the words. I clung to her hands for strength.

"You must understand," she said. "You must take your life from me. Sustain yourself on my devotion. Wherever you are, think of me—here—and live on it."

I promised her that I would. She looked a little anxious then and so I added a phrase or two of sentiment. She seemed relieved.

"If anything were to happen to you—*dearest* Eddie!—I could not bear it. If you do not care for yourself, then care for me."

She seemed to go a little out of focus. I held tight; I concentrated all my will on clearing my vision. The room had begun to tilt. I spoke to her. The room righted itself.

What I said made her happy. She smiled at me with trembling lips.

"Dearest! You do not know—you cannot!—ah, I cannot say it, I do not have the words! Be with me—never leave me! Do not ask me to stay here alone!"

I answered her; she spoke again, then I, then she. I do not remember how long we continued our dialogue. At some point she drew back from me, she released my hands. Even through my fog I could see a peculiar expression on her face. I could not have put a name to it. I saw her rise, go to the bell-pull, tug at it. In what seemed a second only Triphena appeared. The next thing I knew she had helped me to my feet. I remember thinking with odd clarity how very strong she was; I remember being surprised at the fact.

Triphena walked me to the door, she half-lifted, half-dragged me up the stairs. The experience is humiliating only in retrospect; at the time I felt nothing except a growing, urgent nausea. Hurry, I thought. Hurry! But my legs hardly moved; it was a miracle that she got me up as quickly as she did.

She opened the door of my room. I am positive that she gave me a little shove across the threshold. I stumbled in; I fell onto the bed. I rested there a moment before my heaving stomach forced me up. I staggered to the washstand. I retched; I vomited repeatedly. I hung over the basin, shuddering, sobbing, as the painful spasms wracked my body.

I was utterly disgusted with myself. And then, at that instant, I realized what the expression on her face had been: She, too, had been disgusted—revolted.

I have lost her, I thought. She will never help me now.

17

DURING THE NIGHT I managed to struggle out of my costume and into my nightshirt, only to fall back on the bed again, trembling, weak, longing for day to come, afraid that it would come too soon. My head throbbed; my throat was dry and painful. In the darkness I saw myself as I had been since I entered this house—no, since I had arrived in the city. In my mind's eye my image was illuminated by a dreadful light—a harsh, blinding light cast by no natural sun. Its glare allowed me to overlook no detail of my performance; everything I had done was impressed on my brain. I loathed what I saw; I loathed myself. I longed to see Lenore but I had no strength to call her. More—I was afraid that she would sleep undisturbed and that it would be her mother who came to comfort me.

Comfort! I writhed, I cringed, I forcibly obliterated the image of that woman from my thoughts. She loomed up again; I saw every hair, every wrinkle; her luminous eyes expanded, her hands clasping mine, holding me tight— No!

I sat up, soaked in sweat. A brilliant moon had risen. Her light, reflecting on the snow-covered landscape, transformed my room to chiaroscuro. I looked around me, trying to clear my head. What I saw only confused me more. Although I could not be certain, it seemed to me—yes, surely—that I inhabited a chamber whose dimensions had changed. The room was perceptibly smaller than before. I was convinced of it. I looked from bed to bureau, from bureau to window. Had I had the strength, I would have gotten to my feet and paced off the measurement. As it was, I studied the distances intently, struggling to recall the original space. Surely my impression was a trick of light and shade—a deceit of the eye perpetrated by Diana's bewitching glow. And yet—I was not mistaken. The walls seemed to be closing in upon me. The room was shrinking—yes! Unless—

Was I in delirium tremens? Had the alcohol sickened my brain? Surely not so quick—ah, help me!

I flung myself back on the bed, I burrowed underneath the covers like a frightened child. Nothing could have persuaded me to look out. I wanted only the safety, the comforting warmth and darkness of that refuge. Thus I did not hear the door as it opened, I did not hear her footstep as she came to my side. I recall only the stab of terror which pierced my heart as I realized that someone had come, after all, to assuage my fear. Ah, please, let it be Lenore!

Curious—even before I had fully uncovered my head, I was aware of the heavy, sensuous odor of her perfume. Surely no one in this house wore a scent like that. It smelled of the theater, the ballroom, rather than the house

156

of decent gentlewomen. It excited me. I remembered once meeting a woman who wore a scent like that, and she had been— No. No. I struggled to control my thoughts.

Slowly I emerged from the bedclothing. What I saw amazed me. I was too surprised to be frightened.

A vision had seated herself by my side. She had put a lighted candle on my night table. And in the dim and flickering light I saw—no—not a vision, no vision ever gave off such a scent, no vision ever radiated such palpable warmth, no vision had skin so soft to my touch—for she had seized my hand, she had put it at her neck, she had begun to speak to me in tones I have seldom heard—and certainly not from such lips!

My hair was tousled; I put up my free hand to try to smooth it. I arranged my startled features into an expression of pleased welcome. Surely, I thought, I had earned this little respite. I prepared myself to enjoy it. Really, I had been correct in my estimation of her. When she dressed properly—or even improperly, as she was now—she was most attractive. Positively alluring!

She was attired in a silk gown of a pale golden color, and her hair was dressed high on her head in a series of soft cascading ringlets. At her ears, and on her wrists and fingers, diamonds glittered as she moved; her features were accented—no, positively transformed, as I had seen they must be—by paints and powders skillfully applied. Around the neckline—or, rather, the shoulder line—of her dress a soft creamy fall of heavy lace marked the line of her bosom—and yet such was the softness, the richness of the skin beneath, that the lace, the silk, seemed coarse and harsh by contrast, hardly suitable to clothe it.

I realized that I was trembling rather more than I ought if I were to remain in control—that is, if I were to get the maximum pleasure out of this visit, which had come as such a pleasant surprise in the midst of all my failure. How kind of her to want to assuage my battered spirit! Dressed as she was, there could be no mistaking her purpose. The grotesqueries of her paintings were not, it seemed, the only means by which she amused herself! I smiled to myself. So this was why—really why—she had plotted to have me stay!

"Forgive me, dear lady," I said, "but you have taken me completely by surprise. You must give me a moment to . . . ah—collect myself."

She laughed—a soft and infinitely promising chuckle. She had by this time put my hand elsewhere on her person. I struggled to control myself. My head had completely cleared; the walls of the room no longer moved in at me, my stomach no longer heaved, and yet I felt strangely euphoric, strangely giddy. Her perfume, I thought—it is an uncannily powerful scent.

She bent over me so that I was forced to lie back at an uncomfortable angle. I tried to rearrange myself to better advantage. Really, I thought, she is uncommonly quick. She would do better to be a bit more subtle, more tentative. I would have liked a little more time to respond. A woman so attractive, I thought, undoubtedly knows the effect which she produces upon the stronger sex; she should know also, therefore, how to orchestrate that effect so that it produces the maximum impact. But no—on she came, crushing me down, enveloping me, pulling at my nightshirt, undoing God knew what fastenings on her own attire, rushing headlong toward that ultimate moment so frequently desired, so seldom achieved—ah, damn her! Too soon—too soon—the precious fluid spurted from me, it soaked us both and the bedclothing as well.

I turned away my face. She drew back, breathing hard. Her hand moved toward my body but I pushed it away.

158

She sat up straight then and began to pull on her dress. I felt my annoyance rise in me to positive anger. She should not have rushed me. Had she behaved properly—in a more ladylike way—we could both have had our fun. As it was, neither of us was satisfied, and—worse—I had once again failed what seemed now, in retrospect, yet another trial. Would she hold this against me? Would she seek now some petty revenge without giving me another chance?

Without a word she rose and took the candle and left me. I heard the soft thud of the door as she went out. Good riddance, I thought. I was sure that I would lie awake all night trying to think of a way to turn this unfortunate incident to my advantage, but after a time—I do not know how long—I fell into a troubled sleep. I awoke, exhausted, at dawn, but my mind was clear and functioning again. I looked around the room. My heart quickened and then subsided as I remembered my fears of the night before. I had, after all, been mistaken. The room was its ordinary size. It amazed me now to recall my terror.

I sat up. What else? Something caught my eye—something half buried in the rumpled bedclothes. A sparkle—a jewel. I picked it up; I examined it. An earring—the stone dangling from the clip was a full carat at least. So she had come, after all! Rousing from sleep a moment before, I had discounted my memory of her visit. It had been a dream, I thought—an imagined response to my wordless cry. But no. She had been here; she had behaved as I remembered (all too vividly!). I felt the warmth rise to my face as I recalled her presence. Ah, if only she had not been so eager!

I got up; slowly I dressed myself. Every movement of my limbs was an effort. I tried to think calmly about what I should say to Lenore when I saw her. What implications had her actions held for me and my search? Had she been

159

trying to tell me—in such a way!—that she understood her mother's dalliance with me and that she wanted to assure me that she liked—liked!—me for myself? I paused to think of the consequences her actions might hold for both of us. If I aligned myself with Lenore, no matter how secretly, her mother would learn of it. Undoubtedly she would be angry. She wanted no interference in her scheme, whatever it was. Therefore I needed to be very careful. I could not openly encourage Lenore, and yet, as I had seen, I would do well to have her on my side; I could not afford to alienate her.

I slipped the earring into my pocket; I steadied myself against the bureau. Clearheaded as I was, I was still weak. An idea had begun to take shape in my brain; it gave me the strength to continue. I had, after all, been right to be afraid last night; it was simply the object of my fear which had been in error. It was not my bedchamber which had begun to warp beyond recognition: It was I. Mrs. Richmond had got me drunk—she had tried to destroy my will, make me her creature! Very well, I thought; I had intended to play by the strictest rules of etiquette—no, of honor; but if she would not do the same, I felt free to call upon my reserves—my trump card. And yet I would keep my cunning; I would not beg. Last night's encounter with Lenore made me sure of my success. I had to get downstairs; I had to see her, alone, before Mrs. Richmond appeared. (And how I was to face *her*, this morning, I had no idea. I would manage somehow, I told myself; if I worried about our confrontation before it occurred, I would have no strength to deal with it when it did.)

When I entered the dining room I found Lenore just beginning her breakfast. She turned upon me an impassive stare, followed quickly by the most perfunctory of smiles.

160

"You are early this morning," she said. "Did you rest well?"

I do not know which Lenore I expected to see—Mrs. Richmond's daughter or the painted, powdered stranger. She seemed to be her usual self, and yet—did I see a vestige of paint just there, on her forehead? Did her hair seem less carelessly knotted than usual? And her neck—what little I could see of it above the collar of her ecru shirtwaist—did its skin seem more soft, more inviting than before? I could not decide, and I did not want to tire myself by conjecturing. It was a triumph, I thought, that I could face her at all this morning without having my face suffused by the tell-tale blush.

"Tolerably," I said. I felt a little surge of relief. We would, it seemed, be able to converse without constraint. We could simply pretend that her visit to me in my bed had never happened—as, indeed, I would have believed had it not been for the bauble concealed in my waistcoat. Ah, she was clever—but not clever enough for me! I would outwit both of them yet! I reached for the coffeepot. I felt the smile stretch painfully across my face as I filled my cup. Only the sharpest eye could have detected a tremor in my hand as I held the heavy silver urn. "And you?"

"Oh, I always sleep well. It is one of the rewards of an active and busy life."

The conversational avenues towards which this remark pointed were not ones down which I chose to stroll, and so I was silent for a moment, attending to the business of getting some nourishment into my neglected, ill-used stomach. To my surprise, the eggs and toast which I swallowed rested easily there; I found (not unnaturally, since I had not eaten for twenty-four hours) that I was in fact quite hungry. The food gave me strength; when I had cleaned my plate and finished my second cup of coffee, I was able

161

quite easily to inquire if her mother would appear at table.

"I think not. She hardly ever did, for breakfast, before you came. Now she seems to have taken up her old habits once again."

I cast about for the words I wanted to say to her. The knowledge that Triphena might at any moment appear from behind the serving pantry door profoundly inhibited me.

"Can we—if you are not in too great a hurry—ah—could we have a private word?"

She tilted her head at me. "Of course." Not by the slightest hint did she show any reluctance to be alone with me.

"I don't mean here. Triphena will come in—"

"*That* private!" She smiled at me in a friendly way. Was it, I wondered, a cue—an invitation to resume our relationship (relationship!) of the evening before? Surely not now—not here! I was suddenly curious—most anxious—to see what would be her reaction to the little speech I had planned. If she comes at me again, I thought, I will be better prepared to deal with her.

"Would you step into the parlor, then?" she said.

The parlor was the last place I wanted to be. "Ah—isn't there anywhere else?"

Of course there was. As we passed through Triphena's domain I was surprised to see a small pile of food—bread, cold meat—on the table. Triphena stood at the stove pouring a mug of coffee. At Lenore's question, she informed us that a tramp had made an appeal; he waited, now, outside. The morning was bitter cold, the temperature could not have been more than ten degrees.

"You may let him in for a few moments to warm himself if you wish," said Lenore. She cast at me what might have been in another woman—her other self—a sly glance. "We

162

have a good man here to defend us if he causes any disturbance. Most of them are harmless enough."

As we proceeded up the back stairs to her workroom I heard Triphena open the outside door and bid the man enter. I heard his mumbled reply. I hurried on.

Primed as I was with my speech, nevertheless as I entered Lenore's studio I noticed, stacked against the wall, the three wrapped and tied paintings which today she would send to Boston. Only three—and we were left with all the others! Strange, eerie things—but perhaps, after all, they would catch the eye of some collector. I refused to look at the ones which remained; I wanted no distraction, no reminder of the darker side of the personality with which I must deal. I sat on the battered sofa—the climb had exhausted me—and she stood by the window. She looked out, as we spoke, as if now she were reluctant to face me.

"I won't keep you long," I began. "I know you are often away after breakfast—"

"Not always. Not today. A man is coming to fix the floor of the carriage barn and I must stay and oversee him."

"All the more reason why I should not detain you." I paused. I felt like a man who is about to venture, step by careful step, onto a frozen pond during the January thaw. Each advancing footfall, carelessly placed, might be the final, fatal one—and yet there is a prize awaiting him, just there, in the center of the icy expanse, and so he will risk the danger. He will proceed, drawn helplessly on; he cannot turn back.

I wished that she would show me her face. It is very hard to plead to the back of someone's head. One needs interaction with the other to plot one's way.

"You asked me two days ago whether I was succeeding,

163

and I said that my continued presence here showed that I still had hope."

She made no reply, nor did she move so much as a finger.

"Well—if you were to ask me today how I did, I fear that I should give you a very different answer."

Ah—that made her turn to me quick enough! Still she said nothing.

"I am—discouraged," I said. I looked away from her, I looked down at my hands resting on my knees. "I will not succeed. I am sure of it now."

"Why?"

Did she, after all, know what I had had to endure these past days? And had that knowledge been her motive for her midnight visit?

"You must take my word for it. She will never give them to me. It is a fact which, as you can imagine, I have been unwilling to accept. You may call me an optimist if you will—a romantic, helplessly in love with only an idea, a secondhand passion, a furtive glimpse of a life long done. But, for all that, I am not a fool. I know when I am beaten."

"Are you sure?"

"Positive."

I watched her closely. I had of course no idea how my pronouncement would affect her. This was a gamble which I had chosen to make—which I had been forced to make, if you will. Ordinarily I am not a gambling man. I knew, however, that the gambler and I had one vital trait in common—we were both expert dissemblers, adept at hiding our feelings behind our stolid masks. And so, although I watched for betrayals of her emotion, I was careful to reveal none of my own.

"You should give yourself more time," she said. "You

164

are, after all, trying to get at something buried by almost half a century of devotion."

Her words encouraged me. Cautiously I proceeded.

"I have tried to persuade myself to believe exactly that. But it is no good. I am done for."

She stared at me with—I was sure of it—real concern. I sensed her feeling for me then. I felt—yes—her compassion. Excellent! Animal heat was all very well in its place, but what I wanted from her at this moment was sympathy, understanding, a warm and generous feminine heart.

"I should never have come," I said. "It was wrong of me. I have disrupted your lives. I have upset your mother—"

Although it can be an enormous relief to confess one's shortcomings (providing one is sure of hearing a prompt denial), I did not want to continue too far in this direction—this area of the frozen surface where dark and widening lines showed clear danger. And so I drew back and waited. I was positive at that moment—I felt it strongly—that she would say the words I longed to hear, that she would offer—at last—to get for me what I could not get for myself.

"What are you going to do?" she said.

"Why—leave, of course."

"When?"

"Now—today."

"No. Please—"

With inexpressible satisfaction I watched her struggle. She would help me, after all!

"What about—what about that note you sent? To the dealer?"

I shrugged. "I can attend to that as well in Boston as I can here. Better, in fact. I will take the canvases with me when I go."

She shook her head. "You will forget about me if you

165

leave. You will have no further interest in . . . in helping me."

"That is not so. Do you think me so unfeeling that, having raised your hopes, I would then abandon you?"

Very few of us can bear a direct accusation of mean thoughts; certainly she could not. "No—no, I do not think that you would. Not intentionally. But you would go back into your life, naturally you would forget about a casual offer of help made to an acquaintance in a distant city—"

Her voice, as she spoke, had run perilously close to tears. I felt genuinely sorry for her agitation. I stood up; after a moment's unsteadiness I went to her where she stood by the window. I took her hands.

"My dear friend—may I call you that?—be sure that I will not abandon you. But I must go—it is not wise for me to stay. I must acknowledge my failure and leave at once."

Her hands clung to mine. "One more day. Two. I think that you are wrong. I think that she likes you very much. I think that you will succeed—and as you know, I did not always think so. You must be patient."

I wrestled with my irritation. Why, if she so wanted to encourage me, did she not respond to my challenge? She asked too much, I thought; she was not yet willing to do her share in return. But I was determined not to beg; I was determined to play this scene, at least, on my own terms.

I reached for the bauble in my waistcoat. I held it for her. She stared at it as if she had never seen it before; then, without a word, she put out her hand and took it. She studied it for a moment longer and then she slipped it into the pocket of her skirt. She did not—could not?—look at me.

Suddenly she began to cry. Tears ran down her pale cheeks; her mouth twisted into an ugly grimace.

What choice did I have then? Somehow I had to comfort

166

her. I thought that probably she would weep for a little time and then at last she would help me. Awkwardly, hesitantly, I put my arms around her. She was very stiff. The woman in the golden dress might never have existed. I could not believe that they were one and the same. I could not believe that this woman, the previous night, had so aroused me. Had she taken some drug to give her the courage to transform herself? Or had she acted on a desperate gamble, as I had done just now? I murmured something—some incoherent thing. She took a step closer to me and rested her forehead against my vest. I lowered my face to the top of her head; I drew back in annoyance as the growth on my upper lip caught at her hair. I patted her shoulder; her sobs did not lessen, but then again neither did they increase. Given five minutes more, I might have won my gamble; given half an hour, I might have had the papers in my hands.

I never had that chance. As I was about to produce my handkerchief for her, I heard the door open. Although she must have heard it, too, she did not raise her head. But I turned; I looked to see who it was. Perhaps I thought to see the workman standing there, awaiting his instructions.

Instead—God save me from her wrath!—I saw Annie Richmond.

167

18

I DO NOT remember leaving Lenore's studio; I do not remember hurrying down the back stairs and through the
kitchen and dining room and up the front stairs to my own
small chamber. My memory begins when I was once again
alone in my room. My emotions were, curiously, under
control. It seemed to me then that I had lost once for all
any chance of success, but the knowledge of that fact was
not nearly so devastating as I had expected. I found, to my
surprise, that I was able to bear it, and even to think about
it in a calm and rational way.

Still I did not prepare to go. Enough of my former determination—my passion—remained so that I wanted
her—Mrs. Richmond—to send me away. Understand me.
I would have gone at once. I would have accepted her ver-
dict; I would have walked out of that house without a moment's hesitation. But I wanted her to tell me. Call me per-

verse if you will. The power to end our relationship was hers, not mine. And if, even after her anger with me that morning, she chose to allow me to remain, why, I would accept that, too.

Oh, but she was enraged! She put the worst possible interpretation on our embrace. She accused us of conspiring against her, she called us names too dreadful to repeat, she spat at us like an infuriated cat—a lean old hungry cat who sees its dinner snatched away and attacks the dog who steals it. Did she not remember that she herself had offered Lenore to me? Ah—but that was different! That was before I had myself become a delicacy!

I went then, leaving Lenore to deal with her. It seemed the most prudent way. Lenore was, after all, so much more experienced in that line. I sat alone in my room, wondering what they said to each other. At any moment I expected the knock on my door informing me that I was to go. I assumed that Triphena would deliver this message; I hardly expected to see Mrs. Richmond again.

But no one came. After a while I got up and stood by the window, looking out at the bright day. Sunlight sparkled on the snow; through the black leafless trees I saw, below, the dark expanse of the river. I wished that I had a stick of charcoal—the composition of a little sketch would have been a welcome distraction.

A movement near the carriage barn caught my eye. Two people—Lenore and a man—had made their way through the snowy path and now were opening the door. They closed it behind them. I returned to my contemplation of the landscape, awaiting at any moment Mrs. Richmond's order to depart.

It did not arrive. The morning passed. Bored, I picked up a volume of the tales. Towards noon I heard a faint movement outside my door. I waited for a rap but it did not come. I tiptoed to the door; holding my breath, I listened. Nothing. Quickly I opened it. No one. But at my feet was a tray containing my lunch. A wordless reprimand, I thought. She will not tell me to go directly; she will simply isolate me until I leave of my own accord. But I can wait longer than you, I thought. You will need to do more than keep me in solitary confinement if you wish me gone.

I ate; I put the tray back in the hall. The house was quiet. I went to the window. If Lenore had left the carriage house, I had not seen her. I stretched out on the bed. Just before I passed over the edge of sleep I remembered my terror of the night before. I came suddenly awake again. I sat up; I looked at the walls. They were solid and unmoving—unmovable. Relieved, I lay down again and slept.

When I awoke the room was filled with the last reflected illumination of the setting sun. Swiftly the light faded; soon I would be in darkness. It was at this hour every day that I put on my special clothing and went downstairs to deal with her on her own peculiar terms. But not today, I thought. Come and fetch me if you will, but I will not amuse you this day of my own volition.

She did not come. Darkness overtook me. At last I heard the soft noise outside my door again, but again I was too late to surprise the visitor. This time she had brought a lighted lamp as well as a tray of food. They were not altogether heartless, my captors.

I wondered why Lenore did not come to see me. Perhaps she was afraid; perhaps she was—embarrassed. It cannot have been easy for her to deal with the virago who had come upon us in that compromising pose, but perhaps that confrontation had been less arduous than another, now, with me.

Could it be, I wondered, that Mrs. Richmond knew of Lenore's visit to me in my room? Had her anger been directed to that, rather than to our really very tepid embrace in the studio? Surely her wrath had been too great for such a scene?

I did not know. I did not, at that moment, want to know. I could only wait.

I sat for a long time in the glow of the lamp reading the strange narrative of Arthur Gordon Pym. I did not hear the removal of my tray, but when after a few hours I opened my door again, it was gone. I listened—no sound. I stepped out into the hall; I tiptoed to the banister. No sound—all was darkness and silence. It was just past nine o'clock. No light shone under the parlor door. Had they, bereft of my company, abandoned their evenings there? The doors to their rooms were shut, as firmly closed against me as the panel which concealed what I sought.

I felt suddenly very cold—call it a weakening of my heart, if you will. I had never felt more alone, not even that first night at the hotel. Alone—and with less hope than ever of achieving my desire. Ah, why had I come here? For what reason did I stay? I clung to the balustrade and fought against my sudden, my overwhelming despair. I would outwait her—yes—but I needed some way to sustain myself as I did so.

Slowly I began to make my way down the stairs, feeling out each step in the darkness. When I reached the bottom I felt for the wall with my hand and, so guided, found my way to the parlor door. I opened it cautiously, for fear that she was after all within; but if she waited for me there, she did so in the dark. I listened with the acuity of the blind. I heard nothing. I was positive that I was alone.

I advanced into the room. I moved easily in the darkness, as familiar with the arrangement of the furniture as with that in my own home. When I reached the sideboard I found the decanter at once; I remembered its shape and

172

so was able to distinguish it from the others—not many—which surrounded it. I decided against taking a glass as well. A heavy bottle was enough to manage while holding one hand in front of me to navigate my way back up the stairs.

In five minutes I was back in my bedchamber. As I went in I glimpsed a face in my mirror. I did not recognize it. No matter. I uncorked the decanter; I took my first swallow. If the person whom I had seen came back, I told myself, I would deal with him in good time.

I was not, as I have said, a drinking man. Nevertheless, on the day following, the presence of that bottle in my room was an enormous comfort to me. It helped to pass the time; it banished, in fact, the concept of time altogether. I was waiting—for what, for whom, I no longer knew. I had entered a realm where time and purpose no longer existed. The driving passion which had possessed me had gone; in its place was a lassitude which numbed my mind and stilled my ready tongue. Once or twice I seemed about to remember where I was, and why, but at such moments I took another swallow from the bottle and the moment vanished, leaving me at peace again.

So the day passed. The following morning, on my breakfast tray, I found a full bottle of that precious spirit whose warming imbibition had acted so beneficently upon my distress. Clever woman! She knew it all—she anticipated my need. I ignored the plates of food; I seized the bottle, unstoppered it, and drank a long sweet draught. Nothing mattered. I could spend the rest of my life here, I thought, awaiting her summons.

I saw no one during all this time. No solitary prisoner ever had less contact with his keepers. I did not care. They knew where I was; they could come or not—the matter was out of my hands. I lay on my bed and watched the progress of the clouds across the sky; I stood at my window and followed the moon as she silvered the nighttime landscape. I waited.

At last someone came to find me. Of course it was Lenore. She arrived bearing my luncheon tray. The expression on her face when she saw me was not one which I could have described had I been in full possession of my faculties; as it was, I glanced at her for an instant and then averted my eyes, busying myself with taking the tray, putting it on the table, inspecting its contents—it was the usual bountiful display. For lack of anything better to do, I sat down and began to eat. I was aware that she watched me; other than a word of greeting we had said nothing, but I was determined to leave the conversational initiative with her.

Finally she took it. "This has come," she said. I looked up at her, a forkful of chicken pie half-raised to my mouth. She held an envelope. She put it on the tray. I saw that it was addressed to me in care of general delivery, as I had instructed. It was the reply to my note to my art dealer friend. I abandoned my food; I tore it open. I was hardly less anxious than she to know its contents. The single sheet of letterhead bore a few words, hastily scrawled.

Impossible. Are you mad?

I was aware that my hands were trembling. Thoughtlessly I put the paper on the table beside the tray, and before I could prevent her, she had snatched it up.

She went very pale but she made no sound. Something inside her—some life-giving hope, some illuminating spirit—seemed to die just then. She sank onto the corner of the bed, still holding the letter, staring at it but hardly seeming to comprehend it, as I cursed myself and sought

174

to rally my flagging thoughts. I cursed my dealer acquaintance, too. Surely he could have found a more tactful way to decline our offering, Lenore's and mine. Perhaps my own note to him had been clumsily phrased—I could not recall. Obviously I had failed to make him aware of the delicacy—not to mention the importance—of my request. This was a man, mind you, whose establishment I had patronized generously—and this curt, brutal note was my reward. I promised myself sweet revenge on him. Ah, I would do him tenfold the damage he had done to me!

But I had no time for my thoughts. I had the immediate problem of Lenore. What was I to do, now, after all my encouragement of her? How could I soften this dreadful blow? My torpor—my sweet dreamlike state—was upon me still. Desperately I flogged myself into a semblance of brisk cheer.

"Damn the fellow," I said. "I will write . . . ah . . . to Sheridan at once. He's a much better man; I can't think why his name didn't occur to me first—"

She fixed her dull eyes upon me. "No," she said. "No—do not."

"But why? Surely you will not let one rejection—and from such a stupid source—discourage you! This means nothing—nothing!"

She shook her head. "I cannot bear it. It is too painful to think of them looking at my work, criticizing it—"

Of course I understood. The world of the artist is a battlefield, and the survivors wear heavy armor over their souls. The more merciful way, perhaps, would have been to acquiesce and let her work on alone, unrecognized. But I reminded myself sharply of my original purpose in proposing to help her. I had lost (so I thought) my way with the mother; the daughter alone retained the key to unlock—literally—what I sought. Therefore it was the

175

daughter whom I must bind to me by ties far stronger than those of friendship. If I could get her some small success, then she must help me—truly help me—in return, if not at once, then when her mother died. That day, I was sure, was not so very far off. All this was preparation for it.

Driven by the urgency of my thoughts, my brain began to clear. I pushed away my half-eaten lunch; I swallowed the last of my coffee. I moved my chair well away from the table and sat on the edge of the seat, hunched forward, elbows on knees, prepared to wrestle with her fears.

"Of course it is painful," I said. "Your success will be all the sweeter for it. Think—I beg you—of what can be yours."

She shook her head.

"Think . . . of having a life of your own. You are an intelligent woman. You cannot wish to remain buried here when through the slightest effort only you can have recognition for your work. Think—if nothing else—think of the money!"

Ah, there I had her! She showed me such a look then, as would have wrung the heart of a far more callous man than I.

"Yes—money! All yours, to do with as you will. Forgive me—I do not mean to be intrusive—but it is perfectly obvious that if you had sufficient funds, you would be able to have a great deal more enjoyment from your life than you have now. It is too bad that you are so confined. And if you had success, you would be free—"

But who can exhort in the face of such negation? She sat before me, the very picture of gloom, silently denying every optimism which fell from my lips. Although she had not moved, she seemed to be clasping her defeat to her bosom like a wounded child. She cherished this rejection—she clung to it. I was baffled by her mental processes;

176

I was, finally, defeated by them. I fell silent; I reached for the half-empty bottle. She watched me drink. Underneath her expression of obstinate defeat I caught the shadow of contempt.

"It is no use," she said then. "I am not fated for success, any more than you. We have that in common, you and I. We are beaten, we are at her mercy and she has won. Had I left her years ago, I might have gained that strength—that fortitude—which now I lack when I need it most. But I stayed. And you—you, too, have stayed. And you are as defeated as I. She has done for us both. Neither of us will ever get from her what we most desire—I, my freedom, you, your—treasure."

"She cannot live forever."

"Can she not? She will live long enough to beat us both. By the time she dies we will no longer remember why we grudged her life." Her voice was low, but clear and forceful. Each word dropped bitter tears onto my heart. Suddenly she looked at me with purest hatred in her eyes; I was quite startled to see it. "Why did you come here?" she said. "We were all right as we were. Why did you break into our lives and disrupt us? We never harmed you. What right had you to invade us as you did?"

"I was merely seeking—"

"Seeking! And what have you found? An old woman wandering in past dreams? Her daughter waiting out her life alone? I was wrong to encourage you—I admit it—and you were wrong to encourage me. We each sought to use the other, and now we have our reward. She will never give you what you want, and all she has ever given to me is the knowledge that I am a poor substitute, here and now, for the ghosts of her memory. She has bound me to her because she does not love me enough to set me free. She has done the same to you—has she not? Admit it—you

177

have been her slave these past days. She has got you, too, in her stinking web. Do you think that I do not know what she has done to you? Do you think that I do not know about the clothing she forces you to wear—*his* clothing! Yes, they are his!"

Of course I had suspected, but I had refused to think about it. Now, hearing her, I felt my flesh crawl, I shuddered uncontrollably, I reached for my bottle.

"She got them from Mrs. Clemm," she said. "Mrs. Clemm was penniless, of course—she had nothing, not a cent. She came to stay with my mother for a while after he died. Then she went away—I don't know why, perhaps my father forced her out—but she gave the suit to my mother before she left. It was kind of her, I suppose. She could probably have sold it. Certainly she needed the money. I don't know how she managed for the rest of her life. Mr. Dickens gave her a hundred dollars when he made his lecture tour after the war. It was kind of him to do so. Certainly no one here—no American—tried to help her. Even my mother, despite her protestations of love, was unable—or unwilling—to send her any funds, once she had ascertained that Mrs. Clemm had nothing more of value to give her, once she had made sure that she alone had the greatest legacy of all. And she will never—never!—give it to you! Ah, no, she gives nothing, that one! She takes it all, she gives nothing in return!"

She had begun to cry. Weeping, she left me. When she had gone, I took another drink. I thought about what she had said. Of course she had spoken the truth, at least for me. I was, undeniably, defeated. I had danced to Mrs. Richmond's peculiar tune; I had entered as best I might into the shadow-world of her heart. And I had failed. Her last little game with me—her refusal to dismiss me outright—was, I saw now, simply the crowning indignity to whatever shred of pride remained to me. No doubt she expected me to crawl away in secret while she remained to laugh at my credulity, my willingness to play the butt of her outlandish joke. Our last act—the end of our little drama—could continue indefinitely as far as she was concerned. What did she care if I wasted a week, a month—a year, even—here in this confinement?

Anger braced me like a tonic. Very well, I thought, we will end it—now—today. We will take our last tea together, she and I. And when we are done, she will be the winner still, but I will have retrieved that portion of my integrity which she so cruelly sought to steal from me.

At the accustomed hour, therefore, I neatened my clothes—my own clothes—and, fighting off the desire for a sip of brandy to sustain me, went downstairs to confront Annie Richmond for the last time. It did not occur to me to inquire whether she awaited me; I simply assumed that she would.

I was right. She sat in her chair; she smiled at me as I came in. There might never have been a break in our routine, so easily did she welcome me. But by that very ease she betrayed herself. She was not playing charades today, for had she been doing so, she would have reprimanded me at once for my failure to wear my costume. She saw perfectly well that I wore my own things. Presumably, therefore, she was willing to deal with me as myself.

I approached her. I sat opposite her, but I refused the cup which she held out to me. Only then did a shadow fall across her brilliant eyes; only then did her smile falter and fade.

I waited a moment before I spoke; then, unable finally to prolong our mutual suspense, I got out my announcement:

"I have come to say good-bye."

19

SHE DID NOT at first appear to comprehend. She sat quite still, frozen by the abruptness of my words; only her eyes betrayed the agitation of her heart. The fire burned brightly in the grate; the clock ticked noisily on the mantel; the long bare branches of the overgrown yew scratched at the shrouded windows. All was as it had been before, and yet now all was different, for I had come to say good-bye. I was going away. No longer was I a part of this tableau. Once again I was the interloper come to intrude upon their quiet lives. It might all have been a dream. I might never have come—ah, but I had my talisman, my evidence. The growth upon my upper lip remained. I had forborne to shave it off, I did not quite know why. I would carry it away with me and keep it for a while, perhaps—a month, six months—a reminder of my vain folly, my misplaced confidence. Perhaps, I thought, I should keep it as a warning all my life—although never again did I expect to make so monumental an error as I had made in coming to this house.

She moved her lips; she spoke. "No." It was a sigh, a prayer.

"Yes. I must."

"No!" A beseeching cry—a keening for a lost treasure of her own.

"I should never have come. I am truly sorry." (This was not absolutely correct. In time, when I recovered from my chagrin, I would, I knew, regale my hostesses at dinner with the story of my expedition. In time—when I could bear to speak of it.)

Of course she produced her weapons—first the affecting, trembling lips; then the quavering voice; then the shining tears welling up from her eyes and streaming down across her alabaster cheeks. She put out her hand, she clung to mine.

"You cannot leave me now. Not now—not when I have become so deeply attached to you."

"You made it all too clear three days ago that I had angered you beyond forgiveness."

She dismissed the memory with a quick movement of her head.

"A momentary outburst—it meant nothing."

"It meant a great deal to me. I was—I am—convinced that my cause is hopeless. Therefore I must go."

"Please. Stay on a while."

"But why? I have done as you asked, I have obeyed your every whim, I have prostrated myself—literally—at your feet. I have trusted you, I have patiently waited. Now, at last, I realize that I have acted in vain. Nothing will persuade you."

A subtle shift in the focus of her eyes informed me that

182

in her sudden and unpredictable fashion she had gone away from me again. She did not reply at once; she looked beyond me, as she had done before, and I knew that she had entered that shadowy world of the past which, captured forever in her memory, was more real, more precious to her than any event here and now. Her voice, when it came, was breathless and high, like the first tentative notes of the pipes of Pan calling from a distant mountain.

"There was a sorrow in his eyes," she said slowly, "that only I could soothe away."

I did not want to hear. I tried to pull my hands from hers, but she clung tight and I could not get free.

"He used to sit at my feet. He would not speak—it was enough that I was near if he should need me. He used to rest his head against my knee. I looked down at him, I could not believe that it was truly he who sat there."

I gave up trying to escape. She will not continue very long, I thought, and then I can go away.

"He came to me because he needed me," she said. Her voice was a sing-song; its notes reverberated through my head. "He needed comfort, like a mourning child. Of all the women in the world he sought me out. Me! And who was I? I was no one—only myself. At first I could not believe it. I could not believe that he had chosen Annie Richmond. Women longed to meet him. He was besieged with invitations. He refused them all, once he had met me. He wanted no one else. How they hated me, all those others! How they envied me his devotion! His voice—ah, they envied me his voice! He spoke as no one ever spoke before. He could mesmerize a room—a lyceum hall—with that voice. Deep and resonant, thrilling every heart—when he read his poems he inspired a longing to listen forever. I thought sometimes that I would die of ecstasy, listening to that voice! And when he turned his eyes upon me, I was his slave. Any woman was. I could not help myself—I was powerless to resist him. He begged me to love him and I did—I am not ashamed to say it. His lips burned my flesh. I can feel them still. I was completely his. Nothing mattered except the fact that he loved me. I would have done anything for him. I did not care what everyone said—nasty, vicious gossip! I took him to my home—to my parents' home in Westford. My husband could not prevent it. He tried—he admonished me, he even threatened to divorce me. Divorce! As if I would have cared. When Eddie heard of it, he was appalled. He said that he refused to break up anyone's domestic arrangements. I begged him not to go. I swore that I loved him only. I entreated him to take me with him. But he would not hear of it. And people say that he was not a gentleman! He would not hear of it—he refused me on the spot. He went at once. He wrote to me—a long letter in black despair—he told me that in Boston he had taken laudanum. How I wept as I read his words! His stomach expelled the drug and through the mercy of Heaven he survived to suffer on. Yes—that was his life, to suffer. We had no money, he and I, you see. Nothing at all. I said that I would work, I would go into a factory if necessary. He would not listen. He said that he wanted to think of me as he had known me. Tranquil, innocent, sheltered from the turmoil of the world. He said that never in his life had he met anyone who so embodied those chaste and gentle qualities of true womanhood as I did. He did not want his memory of me spoiled, he said, by a vision of me in the workaday world, struggling at so sordid a task as earning money. That was man's work, he said. He could never love a woman, he said, who earned a salary. I would lose him forever, he said, with the first penny I made. Women have a higher function, he said: It is their province to inspire, to encourage, to comfort and console.

What could I do? I was helpless. Either way I had to give him up. He swore he could not live without me. Then he went away. He had his genius, you see, to sustain him. Not to mention Mrs. Clemm. And what did I have? What did he leave to me? Only his memory. Only the sound of his voice in my empty heart. Someone even stole the only daguerreotype I had of him—stole it! I was left with nothing. And yet—do you understand?—I had something, after all. Most women never have as much. Most women never even meet such a man, let alone become his beloved. He put me into his work, do you see? He wrote about me. How many people can say as much? Can you? Of course not. Even as he left—even as I begged him to stay—he was planning out the poem in his head. He did not tell me, of course. That was not his way. He left—he made no promise to return—he went out of my life. And then he died. He died! And I have lived, longing for him, for almost fifty years!"

What could I do? I struggled to hold to my resolve, I fought against the power of her need. No, I said, no and again no! You cannot keep me as your plaything any longer. I will leave you alone with your memories; I cannot revive the dead; I cannot continue in a part which I was never meant to play. But even as I fought this silent battle with my soul I felt my heart begin to weaken. I realized that at last I had a part of what I sought. She had, indeed, reminisced! I had not realized that there was so much to tell. Divorce! Her parents' home! Poor old woman! Well might she mourn losing such a man—well might she cry at never seeing her "Eddie" again! And how had she survived, all these years, with only her memories to sustain her? How many bitter tears had she shed into her pillow? He had died, yes, and left her here alone. And yet, as she said, compared to anyone else she was incomparably the richer, for she at least had had his love. Who could blame her for rushing headlong back into the past? What offered the present to match what once she knew?

She drew back from me. She seemed confused. The room was darker now, the lamps unlit; shadows filled the corners and made a weird landscape of the shabby furniture. She turned to look at me. She saw me now, not some restless spirit from beyond the grave.

"Will you stay?" she said. "Will you comfort an old woman in her last days? I feel very strongly that I have not long to live. No—do not argue with me. I will be glad to die. I will see him again, I am sure of it. We will be together always. And there will be no pain, no sorrow, no parting. Ah, nevermore!"

My heart went out to her. No true gentleman will disabuse a lady of her dearest hope, no matter how vain that hope seems to him.

"Will you stay?" she said again.

My heart melted and gave way. I could not control it. I made no reply. She read my answer in my eyes. Radiant joy suffused her face. She got up from her chair; she stood before me. She tilted up my face. Very gently—it was no more than the touch of a dragonfly's wing—she touched my forehead with her lips.

"You are very kind," she whispered, "to make an old woman happy. And you shall have your reward."

20

AND SO I stayed, and I did my best—I swear it—to make her happy. I threw myself into my role with new fervor, I studied, I wrote, I recited with a kind of genius of my own. Each day we had our hour together, and each day she seemed more pleased with me, more satisfied, more nourished, if you will, by the delights which I put before her. I spent long hours alone in my room preparing for these performances; I rehearsed, I thought, I imagined myself back into his life. Sometimes, rousing from my waking dream, I looked about for Muddie and was alarmed when I did not see her. Poor Muddie! She works so hard for me; faithfully she takes my work to sell where she can. She is completely devoted to me and I to her. What would I do without her? How would I live?

Other times I realized quite well who I was, and where, and still my hand sought my pen, or my bottle, or the furry shape of my beloved Cattarina. I saw her in my mind's eye, sitting for hours at a time on poor Virginia's chest to keep her warm, always purring, never showing a single claw, faithful to the end. But I did not think often of Virginia—the vision was too painful. Virginia is dead. Lucky Virginia. *In pace requiescat.*

Cattarina is dead, too. Starved at Fordham while we were away. Muddie should have taken her in her wicker basket to New York; she should not have left her alone—Stupid woman! She *knew* how I loved Cattarina—knew it, and still abandoned her. I have not forgotten that fact.

The cat here is not so friendly. Several times I have attempted to caress her—how I love to hear them purr!—but she backs away from me; she will not allow me to touch her. Once, catching her asleep on the parlor sofa, I sat down beside her and rested my hand on her stomach. Instantly she was awake, defending herself. My hand was badly clawed before I finally managed to get free. The sight of my blood frightened me. I did not like to see it—I was too forcibly reminded of my mortality. But I have not forgotten the incident. Nasty cat!

Our routine was one of the most felicitous domesticity. In the mornings my breakfast was delivered to my door on a tray. I stayed in my room until lunch time, filling sheet after sheet of the seemingly endless supply of paper. Sometimes I threw away what I wrote, knowing that it would not sell, but usually I was satisfied.

Shortly after noon each day I went down to lunch with the ladies. Or, rather, with the mistress of the house, since the other was rarely home until after tea time. In the afternoon I read—usually alone in the parlor—and at tea I had my sociable hour with my hostess. After a rest, and dinner, the three of us recited to each other from our favorite authors. It was a placid routine—dull, if you will—but peace, placidity, dullness are what I need most. Constant disruption, worries over bills, visits to people who may help me—lectures, even—make any sustained work impossible. I must have my tranquillity.

We were briefly upset one day by the housekeeper's announcement that her sister in Bangor had taken ill with pleurisy. She needed to leave at once, she said, and so she did. We were quite at a loss at first to know how we would manage without her, but soon we worked out a charming little scheme, almost as children play house. By this forced sharing of the kitchen duties we formed ties closer than would have been possible had we remained stiff and formal in the superior role. I do not mind cooking. Many domestic tasks, I find, are soothing to my somewhat excitable temperament. The mechanical motion of peeling potatoes, for instance, is the most delightful work in the world when one's brain is tired from working out the actions of a plot. Heavy cleaning, on the other hand, is no good at all. It exhausts the body to such an extent that the brain cannot function. I never do any heavy cleaning.

These people are wonderfully considerate. They never say anything to trouble me. The reason why I came to them is never mentioned. I think they know that it would upset me so that I could not work.

I will get what I seek, however. Be sure of that. Half a dozen times a day I remind myself that time is passing. I must get on with it. Tomorrow I will ask her again.

Really, they make it so pleasant here that one hates to leave. I remember how I came to this city: the interminable time shut up in the railway carriage, the hotel, the brief explorations of the principal thoroughfare. I feel very tired whenever I think of making the journey back. I must go; I understand that I must. But not until I have achieved my objective. Tomorrow I will ask her again. I think that she might be willing to leave them to me in her will, but do I want to wait that long?

I know where they are. The daughter showed me. A man with a stout iron bar could easily pry open that panel. Do I want to do that? No. I am a gentleman, after all. Gentlemen do not steal.

I am very careful of my appearance. My clothing, old and shabby as they are, are always brushed and neat. She herself, on several occasions late at night, has taken them down to the kitchen to press them after I have taken them off. I leave them outside the door. I never see her collect them. It is very kind of her. She is devoted to me—just like Muddie. I have another suit—gray—but I do not like it. It feels strange when I put it on. No—I always wear the black. The color suits my complexion; it makes me look very pale. Many women are attracted to me; I am sure that it is because of the way I look.

Sometimes I feel that I am growing too pale; I long for a breath of air, the warmth of the sun upon my face. But I cannot leave, even for a moment. I am afraid that they would not let me in again. No—I must stay here, I must maintain my position. But I grow restless, every day I feel more confined. Sometimes, working in my room, I tiptoe to my door and silently turn the handle. It is always unlocked. Nevertheless I feel compelled to test it. One cannot be too careful. The thought of being locked into that small space is intolerable. I know that it would drive me mad.

To calm my mind at such anxious times I construct little puzzles—wordplays, anagrams, or, more often, ciphers. Really, such things are very simple. I often smile to myself to see how people are confounded by them. The key to the (supposedly) unbreakable cipher lies in the principles of language itself—there is no such thing as an unbreakable cipher. Any cryptogram that can be devised by one man can be solved by another.

I have also begun to formulate a theory of national literature based on critical appraisal of our major authors. This will be a long work, book length, as important as *Eureka*. I would let George Putnam have it for twenty-five dollars if he brought out a suitably large edition. He will hesitate at first. He does not like me; he does not like anyone who writes. Like most editors and publishers he is a frustrated writer himself, and he endures with his authors a strange relationship of alternating love and hate which would be amusing if it were not so destructive of the very talent which he says he wishes to encourage. But I will give it to him all the same. He is the best of the lot. Perhaps I can persuade him to lend me ten dollars.

I have kept this long project a secret from my benefactresses. They are most sympathetic to everything I do, but I feel that a long work should be read whole, not piecemeal. Then, too, I am not as sure of the daughter as I am of the mother. Even when she seems in her most cordial humor, she retains an underlying sense of reserve. She is not as wholeheartedly on my side as her mother. It is not that she does not like me. I think she does, very much. But there is something else in her manner—a secretiveness, a propensity to silence, a sense of busy thought whirring behind the stolid face. I do not like that. Several times I have attempted to draw her out, but she rebuffs me. Polite, considerate, understanding, she rebuffs me all the same. She withdraws from us even in our happiest moments together. I do not like such behavior. I feel left out—abandoned.

Her comments on my work, too, are less effusive than her mother's, although, under the circumstances, perhaps that is to be expected. She is always complimentary, of course—but reserved. Even, at times, patently forced. If she thinks that she deceives me, she is mistaken. I have a sensitivity for these things. I know instantly, when I walk into a room, who is my friend and who my enemy. So I am careful with her. I watch her, even as she watches me.

I know that she has a secret life apart from ours. She has—yes!—a solitary vice. I have seen its result hidden in an upstairs room. She locks the door to that room. I know that she does. I have tried to open it and I cannot. But I know what lies within. If she does not soon change her attitude toward me, I will threaten to reveal what she does there.

My hostess—the older one—could not be more charming. Her warmth and sympathy were especially helpful the first few times I read aloud what I had written. Frequently I glanced at her to see its effect. Not once did she fail me. Her beautiful eyes, her warm and tender smile, her soft expressions of encouragement—ah, here was a refuge for the homeless wanderer! She made me feel positively cherished, and for one who has knocked about this cold and friendless world as I have, the sensation was a welcome one, I assure you.

As the days passed, however, I discovered within myself a curious dislike of her predictable praise. Monotonous praise is monotonous, after all. Just for variety's sake, if for no other reason, I would not have minded hearing a little honest demur. But no. Everything I did was always wonderful, marvelous, inspired—surely she could have added a dash of negativism to provide some shade to her constant light? Just a dash, mind you. My sensitive soul can bear no sustained adversity from those who profess to be my admirers. From the outside world, yes—but not from those who call themselves my friends. However, she apparently had no heart to quarrel either with me or anything I did. I began to discount what she said, therefore; no longer did I even hear her effusions. Her vocabulary was limited, for one thing: "superb," "brilliant," "beautiful"—such words become meaningless after a while. If I had had to depend on her for an evaluation of my progress, I should have been in a bad way indeed. Fortunately I knew myself what I did. I needed no one to tell me. Certainly I did not need the uncritical, emotion-laden praise of a woman whose education was as deficient as that of the sex in general. Women are not trained to be critical; they are not trained to make distinctions. They are trained to accept what they are told. On the whole it is a good thing—freaks like Miss Fuller, a prominent frog-pondian, simply prove the general rule.

And I did not, after all, like her the less for her wholesale acceptance of me. She was simply performing her role. Really, she was very sweet. Always, at table, she gave me the choicest cut, the largest slice of pie, the best of the pudding. She was generous in other ways, too: she often put a small present by my place—a handkerchief, an embroidered purse; frequently she gave me books; once she presented me with a truly stunning arrangement of dried flowers which she coquettishly implored me to keep in my room "as a token of her esteem." Of course I complied. One does not, as they say, bite the hand, etc.

I often wonder about her. Has she no life apart from her devotion to me? Monomania is, after all, an indication of an unbalanced mind. It would unsettle me to think that my hostess was deficient in those very qualities upon which, in myself, I place so great an emphasis—clarity, rationality, perception, unerring powers of logic.

And then one day I had a terrible shock, and I knew at last, unquestionably, that I had been right to wonder about her fixation. It happened this way:

We had had our usual convivial dinner; we had spent our usual time afterwards entertaining each other. I had been in particularly good form that evening, I thought. My hostess had been moved to tears—and then to tears of laughter—as I read from *David Copperfield,* and when I had done she presented me with a touching speech upon my powers of dramatic reading. Her emotion was perfectly simple and sincere, and with equal sincerity I accepted her sentiments. Really, at that moment, I was quite fond of her. Since the hour approached ten o'clock we parted then without attempting to begin anything new. As we climbed the stairs—the three of us—she laughed gaily to herself as if she held some delightful secret. Just before we reached the top she turned to look back on me, two steps below (her daughter had preceded us; we were alone). She smiled at me; she positively bubbled over.

"There is something for you in your room," she said. "Do not be alarmed—I did not want you to be frightened, that is why I mention it to you now instead of letting you come upon it unawares."

Somewhat mystified, and not a little curious, I thanked her. She went into her room and I went on to mine. I opened the door; I held in the light. I do not know what I expected to find. Often my imagination far outruns any earthly possibility.

I saw it at once. My heart wrenched painfully in my chest. My knees went weak. I clung to the door. I heard my cry of terror.

Perched on my bureau, waiting to fly at me, its eyes glaring red, its feathers lustrous black, its talons cruelly curved, its beak ready to tear at my flesh, was the awful bird of night, my secret thoughts given shape, the shape I feared most to see—and she knew, she *knew* my fear—of the subject of my greatest success, of the albatross to my fame from whose shadow I struggled to emerge—of the midnight caller: the Raven!

21

THEY HAVE played a monstrous trick upon me. No—not the feathered corpse of that malevolent crow, although that, God knows, was monstrous enough. No—worse than that. Infinitely worse.

They put something into my coffee. Or my brandy, or my tea. They slipped it in—some pernicious drug whose effect upon me was worse than death itself. Ah, better that I should have died at once than live with this hideous knowledge!

I am not responsible. Still—I acted, I did those things; I must live on with the knowledge black in my heart. Ah, what have I done!

We sat as usual at our dinner. I felt strange. I suppose I showed it. My ears buzzed, my head whirled. I smiled foolishly at everything they said. We chuckled over the bird. I said I did not mind it. They were pleased. She shimmered in the glow of the lamps. She seemed to have a kind of golden haze around her. I fixed my eyes upon her. I felt that to lose her from my sight was to lose everything. The walls of the room wavered; I could not look at them. They seemed to move—to be closing in. I shook my head. It did not clear. She leaned toward me. She smiled at me. Everything was in that smile. Everything! I knew its meaning as I had never known it before. Even as I strugged to focus my burning eyes I felt my heart grow cold. Her beauty was at that moment an ominous thing which seemed to lead me on to some dreadful rendezvous. Silently I resisted. My fear rose up against my will. It escaped me; it filled the room. Why was I here? What would become of me?

We finished our meal. We rose. We went across the hall to the parlor. I saw that we were alone, she and I. I looked around for the daughter. I asked for her; I begged to know where she had gone. As cold and distant as she was, that daughter, I knew that she had her own strict code of honor—and, having it, would protect mine. I felt that to spend another minute alone with my hostess would be my damnation. I felt that I had to escape. I stood by my chair; I was afraid to sit down. The room tipped and tilted, the walls heaved. She spoke to me. She tried to entice me to sit with her. I drew back; I held fast to the carved wooden back of the chair. I felt the sharp edges digging into the flesh of my hand. Her eyes glowed at me. Her voice was the siren's song. I tried to speak but I could not. I willed her to keep away, but my will was a broken, useless thing; it had no force.

She came at me. Her mouth moved, her hands stretched out to take me. Get away, I shouted, leave me; but still she came. The room darkened, only the fire burned bright, its heat filled my trembling body, suffocating me until I felt that I must tear the stock from my throat before it strangled me. But my fingers had no strength, I could not get it off. Softly she spoke to me; softly she touched the binding cloth, unwrapped it, freed me. I felt that if her fingers touched my face, my neck, I would scream, I would push her violently away. I tried to defend myself from her advances but I was helpless. Helpless! The effect of the drug had left me totally in her power, my body debilitated, my senses painfully acute.

Her fingers fiddled at my shirt. I turned my head to avoid her hypnotic eyes. My agitated glance fell onto a dark feathered shape perched on the mantel. There it sat, waiting, watching—ah, no! I shut my eyes to escape its stare. I heard my feeble protestation. I felt myself sink to the floor. I felt her hands upon me. I surrendered myself to that agony.

* * *

I awakened in the night—pitch black, cold—conscious of my unclothed body trembling in a bed—my bed? I had heard, in my stupor, the anguished moaning of a soul in torment. I had thought to go to help it. Who cried so, here in this house? Who wept, who perished?

I listened. I heard it still. My throat ached, my lips were dry and painfully cracked. The sound filled my ears. I writhed in my bed. My hands hurt dreadfully—throbbed with pain. My hands! Why? I moaned, I cried, I begged for someone to come. I might have been alone in the world, the last survivor of a deadly plague. Perhaps they had locked me in. Did they think to save me? But I must get out. I must escape—

I heard a new sound then—the soft click of the door knob. A shaft of light sliced into the darkness. A figure stood there, looking in, silhouetted against the dim glow of

197

the hall lamps. A woman's figure, advancing toward me, looming over me. Had she come to rescue or destroy?

She sat beside me on the bed. In the faint light I saw her face. She made no move to touch me. She simply watched me warily, and yet not without concern. At last she said, "Are you feeling better now?"

I asked her for some water. She took a glass from the night table and held it to my lips. The effort of sitting up and drinking quite exhausted me. I sank back again and gathered my strength.

"There," she said. "You had us quite worried, Mother and me."

"I don't remember."

She watched me. "Don't you?"

"No."

"What do you remember? When does your recollection stop?"

I tried to comply. "At dinner—I felt—uneasy—"

She watched me. "Were you angry?"

"Angry? No—no. Why do you say that?"

"You have no memory at all of what happened?"

I tried very hard. "We ate—we went into the parlor—I felt unwell—"

"Ah." She nodded at me. "We will put it down to fever, then." She laid her hand on my forehead. "Yes—you are still warm."

I moved restlessly under her touch. "Put what down? What—happened?"

She removed her hand. "You were distraught. She knew of course that you were not yourself. I do not think that she will hold it against you."

"Hold what? What do you mean?"

She put a warning finger to her lips, and I knew then that I had spoken too loud. I had not been aware of it. I started to apologize but she gave me no chance.

She felt down along my arm to find my hand. I cried out as she touched it. She took it up; she bent her head low and examined it.

"You have been badly clawed."

The fear which had begun to recede came over me again stronger than before. I struggled to speak. She watched me. "It was not of course the cat which angered you so. The animal was merely the unfortunate recipient of your—ah—passion."

I flexed my fingers. To my horror I felt fresh blood begin to flow. I heard my whimper. I cannot bear the sight, the feel of blood. Frantically I wiped my hand on the sheet, but the more I tried to staunch the wounds, the more they bled. My hand scrabbled there amongst the bedclothing like a thing separate from myself.

"Please tell me," I said. "I must know. I cannot bear not to know."

"You were not responsible. For whatever reason, you were not responsible. I understand that, and I am sure she does also."

"What? Please—"

She stilled my hand by taking it in her own. She waited for a moment until I had calmed a little; then: "You behaved, last evening, in an ungentlemanly fashion. You—made advances, shall we say?"

"I made— How? What happened?"

"You—ah—tried to force yourself upon her."

I heard her voice quite clearly, but I could not understand the words.

"Please do not ask me to be more explicit," she said. "A person of your sensitivity can understand how painful it is to discuss one's own mother—"

"Please. You must tell me. What did I do? I must understand. I shall go mad if I do not understand—"

"She suffered only slight bruises on her arm and wrist.

199

Her dress was a little torn. She told me that you had seemed slightly ill at ease, and that she had thought to retire directly to allow you to rest, but you insisted upon sitting in the parlor as you always do, and so she tried to humor you. Very quickly you became distraught, she said. She tried to calm you by loosening your cravat. Instead of calming you, her action only inflamed you. If it had not been for the cat—"

Gently she put down my hand. "She struggled with you. And the cat—really, it is most extraordinary—the cat literally leapt to her defense, like a dog to the defense of its master. The cat jumped onto your back. You tore it off, your attention thoroughly diverted from my mother. You held the cat up high. It hissed and spat and clawed you dreadfully. You held it by the neck. Tighter and tighter. My mother said she heard a little *snap!* The cat stopped its noise. Then you realized what you had done. You threw it down. In that instant my mother ran out. I was just coming in. She almost collided with me in the hall. She told me what had happened. I went into the parlor with her. I helped her to get you upstairs."

I lay still; I succumbed to the erratic pounding of my heart. Its rhythm possessed me. I felt that if I moved, if I spoke, I would arrest its movement. I would die. Here, in this house, far from my accustomed life, I would die.

I believed what she told me only because I could not refute it. I had no memory, no proof—ah, what had driven me to behave so? What demon had possessed my soul and turned me into a raging madman?

I realized that she was speaking and that I had missed her first words.

". . . to forget this night," she said. She laid her hand on my shoulder. Her smile expressed her deep sympathy; gazing at it, I experienced an almost unsupportable sense of relief. Truly, she would help me if she could! "I will stay with you," she said. "I will sit there, by the window, and watch. No one will harm you. You can rest undisturbed. In the morning all will be as it was before. No one will chastise you. Do not be afraid. Go to sleep."

She rose from my side. She pushed shut the door until only the faintest line of light showed at its edge. In the darkened room I saw her black shape move to the chair by the window. The heavy beat of my heart shut out all other sound. I could not hear her breathe; I could not hear the rustle of her dress as she moved. My ears filled with the sound of my own body's life, and yet I did not feel alone. I knew that she was with me.

I do not know how long I lay quiet, waiting for sleep to come. Perhaps five minutes, perhaps an hour. Gradually I relaxed; gradually I was able to think of what she had told me. And it seemed to me now that what she had told me was in error. How? I did not know. But what she had told me—what her mother had told her—was, I knew now, in-correct. It had not happened that way.

Tension ebbed from my body; my heart subsided. My brain revolved, slow and steady, around the action which I had performed but could not remember. What had hap-pened? What was happening now? Were this room and this silent companion a dream still? Were they part of the same dream perhaps? Had I done with raving, or would I spring up now with new strength and leap upon her, too?

Where was my bird? It had seen all—heard all—ah, speak to me, black witness, and tell me what I did!

As if in answer to my plea I heard just then a voice— whose, I could not tell; it resembled no voice I knew—and as I listened I felt my fear come on again; I felt the heavy smothering weight of it on my heart, I weakened, I trem-bled, I lay helpless before it and cried out to it to get away.

I cried out; there was no sound. I cried out; no one came; she did not come. I was alone in the dark, abandoned.

Her hands were upon you, said the voice.

No.

She has had her way with you, and you are done for, said the voice.

No.

She will abandon you now. Evil destroyer! She has destroyed you!

No.

She has used you as she would. You are nothing to her now.

No.

Worse than nothing—she must put you away now. She will have no witness to her crime.

No.

She must! You are a danger to her now. She must be rid of you!

No.

Run away! Save yourself! Go back—go quickly!

"No!"

With that cry my consciousness fled. Darkness and silence enveloped me; I knew nothing more.

22

My NIGHTMARE vanished with the coming of the sun and I awoke peaceful and alone and filled with a steady resolve. I knew exactly who I was, and where, and why. And I knew, too, that I must go away—now—this morning. I must accept my loss of something I never had a chance to possess. I must return to my own life. I must forget this strange journey, this treacherous whirlpool in the placid stream of my existence.

I longed to see Muddie again. Had she, I wondered, sold "The Bells?"

I lay quiet and watched a spider dangling from her thread near the window. In the closet were my clothes—my own clothes. Soon I would arise and put them on and go downstairs to say good-bye.

My hands were stiff. I lifted them; I looked at them. Someone had bandaged them. How had my injuries occurred? A little blood from the right hand had seeped through the cloth—a dark and frightening stain. Still, injured hands need not prevent my departure. They hurt hardly at all, but I remembered that last night—

Last night—someone tried to—what? I could not remember. I recalled only that familiar sense of fear, of persecution—ah, why do they hate me so? Only Muddie is truly devoted to me. Bless her. And Sartain, of course. Sartain is in Philadelphia. He cannot help me now. I must go to see him.

Why does Muddie tell these women that I will edit their miserable poems, prepare them for publication? She makes agreements for me which humiliate me, degrade me, reduce me to hackwork—worse than that. She sells my favors to the highest—to the only—bidder. She bargains away my only negotiable stock as a critic—my integrity. Still, we are so desperate for money that to turn away one hundred dollars—my most recent gratuity—would be unthinkable. Poor Muddie!

I got up. I dressed. I listened—no sound in the house. It was a brilliant day, sun in a blue sky, blinding reflection on the snow. A good day to travel. Softly I opened the door of my room; I saw no one. I came out into the hall; I went downstairs. There is a curious portrait hanging at the landing. Often I have stopped to inspect it, to puzzle over it, but I did not do so now. I wanted nothing to delay my progress.

A faint *chink* of cup on saucer from behind the closed dining room door alerted me to the presence of someone inside. I paused. Might I do better perhaps to go unseen, unheard—most assuredly unmourned?

But before I could act on this wiser course my hand was perversely on the knob, and in an instant I had opened the door and revealed myself to those within.

204

It was, after all, only Lenore. She looked up and nodded at me and bade me enter. Well, I thought, and why not? At least they can give me breakfast before I go. They have used me badly. They can do no less than fill my stomach now.

I sat at my place. I poured a cup of coffee; I helped myself to a portion of burned scrambled eggs. My movements were awkward, I held my fork with difficulty. She did not speak to me again until I had eaten my food and poured a second cup of coffee. Then, turning upon me a gaze disturbingly intent, she said, "What will you do now?"

"Go, of course."

"Must you do that?"

I am not ordinarily at a loss for words, but now I held my cup halfway to my lips and thought for some reply and tried once again to understand the peculiar workings of her brain.

"Yes," I said at last. "I must. Of course. What would you have me do?"

She did not answer me at once. She stood up and walked cautiously to the door, opened it, looked out into the hall, and then shut the door again firmly and came back to the table. She pulled her chair close to mine; she leaned forward and lightly touched my bandaged hand.

"I would have you stay," she said. Poor Lenore! How painful for her to make such a declaration, how embarrassing to know that it will be denied. I tried my best to protect her feelings; a gentleman could do no less.

"Dear lady—why?"

"I think that you may be very near success," she said. "I am sure of it. You need only stay on a little while longer."

I felt my heart beat heavy in my breast. I did not want her to speak so. I did not want to be reminded of the unhappy history of my stay in this house. I had thought, this

205

morning, to put it all behind me. Now she was tearing the scabs from my soul's wounds, she was exposing me once again to the agonies of my obsession.

"You have said that before," I replied. "You were wrong then; why should I suppose that you are not wrong now?"

"Because. Last night—"

I shook my head sharply; I held up my hand to forestall her words. I did not want to hear. Last night had been a horror. I had buried it in my memory. I did not want to think of it again.

"Very well," she said. "I will not speak of that. I will speak of something else instead. I will ask you for your help." Her voice was soft and most appealing.

I had been carefully brought up always to defer to the gentler sex. And so, despite my misgivings, I waited to hear her out. She took my hesitation for encouragement.

"You must understand that I am perfectly sincere," she said. "I have thought very hard of what I am to say to you. This is not an easy request for me to make. But you are the only one who can comprehend my difficulty—our difficulty, if you will." She paused. I made no reply. She continued:

"We must put her out of the way."

Her words fell one by one into the abyss of my heart. I looked away from her; I could not bear to meet her eyes.

"Do you see?" she said. "*She* is the source of all our trouble. She keeps us here at her pleasure, she plays with us in her cruel game. If she were gone—"

As much as I dreaded her words, I dreaded more her silence. I faced her once again, and she responded to my unspoken appeal.

"If she were gone we would both be free, you and I. You would have what you seek—yes, I swear you would—and I—I would have the means to live what remains of my life."

I asked a stupid question then—stupid, because I knew the answer before I spoke.

"But where would she go?" I said.

She made no reply—needed to make none. I was conscious then that my injured hands had begun to throb; that my mind, which had seemed so clear, had begun to cloud again, to hum with forbidden thought. I shook my head sharply, repeatedly, trying to maintain my fragile hold on my resolve.

"I remember you when first you came to us," she said. Her voice had changed—it was warmer now, more intimate, as if she sought to quiet the fears which just now she had aroused. I longed, suddenly, to let her comfort me; if I listen to her, I thought, she will tell me what to do. I realized that I was tired—too tired to think, to plan—"You were so bold," she said. She smiled a little. "Really, it was quite entertaining to see you. You were bold—and terribly in earnest as you so shamelessly lied to us. You quite endeared yourself to us. No one had ever come to us with quite such a clever story—although of course it was not so clever after all, was it? And I needed to test your devotion—your determination—to see if you would return after your first defeat. And you did—you did! You did not fail me then. Do not fail me now. You must not think that I did not understand your feelings. I did—I do still. I respect you enormously. You have tried very hard. I know how important your journey was to you. It was the passion of your life, was it not?"

Slowly I nodded; I dared not speak. My tears, barely withheld, would have been humiliating beyond endurance.

"I understand what it is to have a passion," she said. Her voice mesmerized me; I felt myself succumb. "We are very much alike, you and I. Do you know that? And so now I ask you to help me—to help *us*—and then we can both go free. She is a very old woman, after all. She has lived her life. She has no right to deprive us of ours. I have watched her, these past days, tormenting you until I can no longer bear the sight. You are too fine to be subjected to such indignity. It is not easy for me to speak so of her—you know that. I see that you do. You know everything. I do not have to explain to you. You know what she is. You know what she has. I have planned it all. You have only to do as I say. Nothing can go wrong. Will you help me?"

I nodded again. I was totally hers. All my fierce longing had returned. Once again I surrendered myself to the ecstasy which I had thought to banish. Once again I felt the hot excitement of my chase; once again—ah, sweet pain!—I allowed myself to imagine them, to see them, hold them, read every precious word.

Her voice went on, steady, hypnotic, binding me to her purpose with chains far stronger than any forged by human hands. "She will rest in her room today. I will carry up her meals. At noon her lunch, at four o'clock her tea, at six o'clock her dinner. At eight I will ask her to come down. I will tell her that I have a surprise for her. She will not refuse. I will need you then. Be ready."

She fixed my eyes with her own. I clung to that look— the only refuge for my turbulent spirit. Long—long and fast we remained so, binding my faltering will to her strength, swearing a silent oath of fealty for the final trial. I was her tool, and she my cunning operative.

At last she bade me go. Like an automaton I walked out, I traversed the hallway, I climbed the cavernous stairs, I paced the distance down the corridor to my cell. Every footfall was like the muffled fall of earth upon the casket. And I—ah, help me!—I, entombed, was still alive to hear.

23

BLOOD EVERYWHERE—ah, wash me, make me clean!—
blood on the floor, on the walls, on the chair where she
had sat. Blood on me, on my hands, my face, the good
gray wool of my suit. Blood across my eyes—I saw the
nightmare scene as if a film of gore obscured my vision, I
acted out my maddened role in a fog of murderous crimson.

I do not think she suffered any pain. We were too quick,
we sprang upon her before she knew, we held her fast before she could cry out. We stifled her mouth before we
plunged the dagger in. She gave a violent wrench, one fu-
tile attempt to save herself, and then she fell back and our
work was done.

Done? Hardly! What now must we do? How can we explain? The authorities, the police, the neighbors—someone will suspect! The deed had been done so quick that I

had had no time to hesitate—but now, done, it seemed a monstrous crime, a foul violation of my deepest self-control. No sooner had she fallen lifeless from my grasp than I began to fear the consequences of my action. Oh, how I trembled! How I staggered under the weight of that knowledge!

I looked about me to escape. Run, I thought, run and run, do not delay, get away from this incriminating scene, do it now while you still have time. No one will know that you were here. But even as I turned to act upon my thought the daughter seized my arm and held me fast. I could not make her understand my fear. She would not listen. Instead she fixed me with her iron gaze and instructed me to pull the dagger out. I tried to obey her but I could not, I could not touch it again. She was annoyed with me; I could see that she was, but it made no difference. I would rather have died than touch that weapon. With an exclamation of contempt she took it out herself. Carefully she dropped it on the floor. I saw that it was not a dagger after all, but an ordinary kitchen knife. Without a moment's hesitation she produced a coarse sack and, dropping into it a pair of silver candlesticks and the silver tea service from the side table, beckoned me to follow her out of the room. I could not believe that we were to leave the body so. But I went after her; I did not question or argue. We closed the door behind us and stood alone in the dimly lighted hall. Alone! While behind us lay that unspeakable thing—that damning consequence of our separate desires!

She bade me follow her into the kitchen. I did so. She took a glass from the sideboard—a glass already filled with a cloudy, whitish liquid. She bade me drink it. I did so. She picked up a cloak from a hook by the door and threw it around her shoulders. Never had I seen her so—dare I say it?—so alive. Her eyes glowed with a steady purpose; her expression was calm, yet fired with a reflection of inner triumph. The sense of passion repressed, of life thwarted and denied, had vanished. She was a new woman. I hardly recognized her.

She told me that she was going out to dispose of the sack of silver. I protested. I did not want to be left alone. No—worse than alone. I did not want to be left with *that*. It would walk, I was sure that it would walk. It would spring at me from behind the closed door.

She had anticipated my fears, she said. Hence the drink which she had given me. Be calm, she said. The drug will take effect very quickly; you will sleep the night through without awakening. Go upstairs, she said. She came up close to me; she stared at me. I had no choice but to obey her.

I hurried through the hall. I did not look at the parlor door. I willed myself to get past it. I climbed the stairs without once glancing back. I did not even tremble, so firm was my faith in her commands. The drug must have begun to take effect by then, because I was conscious of a growing sense of peace—of the ebbing of my fears, the beginning of a sense of satisfaction, the first faint tremor of new hope. What was done was done—now at last I would have my treasure.

I went into my room. Carefully I removed my clothing and put them outside my door. I sank onto my bed and fell asleep.

24

OF COURSE she had to tell the police. And of course they had to come to investigate. I never saw them. She told me to hide in the crawlspace above the carriage barn. I was glad of the refuge. I wanted nothing to do with the police. They stayed that morning for what seemed like many hours—I suppose it was two or three—and when finally they left, they warned her that they would undoubtedly return.

She summoned me down then, and we ate a hurried lunch in the kitchen. She had told the police, she said, that during the evening she had been visiting with a family on Cabot Street. She could produce at least a dozen witnesses, she said, to prove that she was there. She stayed late. When she arrived home she found the hideous scene in the parlor. The back door had been left open; certain valuable items had been taken. A particularly persistent tramp had visited the house a week or so before, she said; the neighbors would confirm it. He had seemed at the time to be oddly slow, reluctant to leave, as if, she said, he had been summing up the house and its occupants for future reference. She had not realized at the time why he acted so. But obviously, she said, three women alone—two, now that the housekeeper had gone—were a tempting target for a thief.

She should not have left her mother alone, she said. She realized now that she should not. If she had dreamed that any danger existed—but who would have thought it? Even though the newspapers reported almost daily the hordes of beggars traveling from door to door—people thrown out of work by the recent crash, or people too lazy to work in the first place—still, one felt reasonably safe. Or at least until now.

She leaned against the sink counter as she spoke. I heard her voice tremble. I saw her wipe away a tear—one of many which she had, I was sure, produced for the police. I perched on the edge of the worktable and sipped my good hot coffee. The barn had been unbearably cold, and I was shivering still.

The undertaker—a Mr. Richardson—had taken away the body, she said. She herself would clean the room that afternoon. The police had given her permission to do so. Already they had sounded the alert for the suspicious tramp. Of course they would check her alibi also. She was not concerned. They were her good friends, those who would vouch for her, and they would stand by. She had no worries in that direction, she said. No—I was the worry. If we were to succeed, I would have to stay hidden. We must carry out our plan, she said. She had decided that I must spend my days in the crawlspace for as long as the police investigation continued.

Immediately I protested. It was impossible. There was not even room to stand up. It was a cold, dark, miserable place. I was sure I had heard rats. Impossible—she could not ask it of me!

She did not ask—she commanded. We had no choice, she said. For a few days only. At least until after the funeral.

A peremptory pounding on the front door interrupted our debate. A look of alarm—the first fear she had shown—passed over her face.

"Quick!" she said. "Do as I say! I will admit them. Listen at the hall door. When you have heard me take them into the parlor—the moment you hear me close the parlor door—run to the barn and conceal yourself."

She went then to answer, and I remained to do her bidding. The heavy clump of their feet in the hall intermingled with the beating of my heart. I heard their voices—rough, loud, masculine voices, answered by her calm clear tones. I heard the parlor door shut behind them. I turned away then; I ran back to my hiding place.

I do not know, now, how many days I stayed there, wretched, shivering, my bones aching with the cold. Days and days—I lost all count. At night I came down, I crept into the kitchen where she fed me my supper, and then I went to my room and stretched out on my bed and waited for the morning, when I must return to my prison.

The callers who interrupted us that first day had been reporters, not the police we feared. But reporters were dangerous, too: one false word and they were at one's throat. We—*she*—needed to be very careful with them. Apparently she managed them well. She showed me the newspapers which carried an account of the death, and while they understandably gave it a large play for a day or two, they gave no hint of anything other than what had become the official line: "Shocking crime," "Police search for tramp"—all perfectly according to her plan.

The day of the funeral came and went. A few people came to pay their condolences—I never saw them, of course—but many of Mrs. Richmond's friends and contemporaries had died, and so not as many came as might have been expected.

For that we were thankful.

Inevitably, interest in the case subsided. New crimes were committed; the attention of the police was diverted. Sometimes, crouching in my frigid refuge, I amused myself by working out a new adventure for Dupin. I imagined him coming here, to this city—to this very house—called in, say, by an old friend who has a nephew attached in some way to the local police. The nephew's career is at stake if he cannot solve this horrible crime; but he is baffled, everyone is baffled, the murderer cannot be found. Dupin accepts. He is ready for a little vacation; he has never seen America; he will travel in a leisurely way, pausing to visit Washington and New York and Boston before coming here. He arrives. The authorities acquaint him with the details of the case; he comes to the scene of the crime, he examines everything, he listens to everyone, he thinks about what he has seen, about what he has been told, and in no time at all—*Voilà! C'est la fille et l'étranger qui sont les sauvages.*

No—no. I must not imagine such absurdities. I shuddered uncontrollably; I pulled my greatcoat more closely around my shoulders. Dupin did not exist. I felt that it was important to remember that fact. Dupin died with his creator. No one would come, now, to expose us. The trail grew colder each day. Surely we were safe. We had only to wait. Everything would proceed according to plan.

One evening, examining my hands, she told me that I

216

need wear the bandages no longer—and then, almost as an afterthought, she said that the will had been probated. I flexed my fingers; I congratulated her on her new wealth.

"Oh—I am not to have so very much," she said.

My long confinement had slowed my brain. I did not at first understand.

"But—then why endanger yourself? Why endanger *us*?"

"That is the point," she said. "If I had benefited largely, I would never have dared take the risk."

Although I knew that my question was rude, still I felt emboldened to put it. "How much?" I said.

"About a thousand a year."

"And the rest—"

"To charity. It is all quite safe, you see."

"And are you content?"

"Of course. One can live quite well on a thousand a year, and yet it is not so large a sum as to arouse suspicion. I think that I will travel for a while—everyone will understand."

"Did she—did she mention specifically what I—"

"No. The phrase was, I believe, 'all the rest, residue and remainder.' To me, of course."

We faced each other across the remains of our supper. A kerosene lamp bathed us in its unsparing illumination. I saw every line in her face, every blink of her expressionless eyes. The corners of the room—we were, as usual, in the kitchen—were dark. The latched shutters forestalled any glimpse of us—of *me*—from outside. In concealing my presence, as in everything else, we had been successful. The police investigation had been, I thought, remarkably sloppy. They had given the carriage barn only the most cursory examination, and they had never even bothered to explore the crawlspace. Nor had they found the bag of silver which she had hidden—where, she never told me.

217

I realized that some moments had passed since her reply. I was aware that the question of time—how fast, how slow—had become a mystery to me during the past weeks. I could no longer tell when, say, an hour had gone by, although formerly I was very good at such calculations. In other ways, too, I felt that I was failing: my eyesight, for instance, because of the gloom of my daytime concealment, had weakened considerably. To sit in the glare of the lamp was very painful. My eyes watered and ached. And yet I needed to stay with her, just now—I could not yet, this evening, go upstairs to my room, to lie on my bed in the comforting darkness. I needed to ask her an important question. For a moment it eluded me. What was it? I am sure that my face did not betray my confusion. Ah—yes. Now I remembered. I put up my hand to shade my eyes.

"When do I see them?" I said.

The imp of the perverse preys on us all. "See what?" she said.

O gentle lady, do not toy with my deepest—my only passion! Not now, not so far along in our game! My hand trembled before my eyes; I exercised all my power to hold it steady.

"Ah," she said. "Of course. How could I have forgotten? Do not look so. You shall have them. But we must wait. We can do nothing precipitous. Everything depends on the ordinary way. Nothing unusual must happen. Believe me, you shall have them."

What could I do? Short of smashing open the hidden compartment in the bookcase, I was helpless—totally at her mercy. If I made any trouble for her, she had only to report me to the police to put me out of her way. She could tell them, for instance, that I had brutalized her, frightened her into concealing me. Of course they would believe her. She was a respectable lady of good family, well-known

218

in the community. I was no one—an outsider who had intruded myself into this house under highly suspect circumstances. I would have no chance at all. I had to obey her; I had to wait.

I left her then and went upstairs to my room. The house was dark and quiet. I thought of our former evenings, gathered together in the parlor after supper to read aloud, to converse in a civilized way. I longed for an hour of that companionship now. I longed—yes!—to see the face of that one who had held what I most desired. I would have given the rest of my life, just then, for one smile, one word of affection from her. But she was dead. And I—

Ah, what had I done! Did *he* know? Had he watched as his beloved left this life? Where was she now? With him? Did they both see me here, climbing these dark stairs, making my lonely way to the chamber where I slept?

I felt cold tears upon my face. Had I betrayed him by my actions? Had I, in seeking to prove my devotion, committed the irrevocable act which branded me for all time his foulest enemy?

I staggered under the weight of my remorse—my total desolation. Ah, what had I done? And what must I do still?

25

WE CONTINUED in our game of hide-and-seek for some days more, and then at last one morning she told me that I need no longer conceal myself. She had heard, she said, that the tramp in question had been seen in Lawrence. The police expected to pick him up that day. He would deny everything, of course, but no one would believe him. He was the perfect suspect—poor, friendless, alone, with no one to substantiate his protests. The case would be closed—or, at least, the intensive investigation would cease—and we could resume our lives. The public would be satisfied; the police and the newspapers could turn their attention to other, more immediate concerns.

There was a window above the sink counter. She walked to it, she pulled up the blind. She pushed up the sash, she unlatched the shutters. The morning sun flooded in. Although snow still covered the ground, the air this day was mild—a foretaste of spring. Soon the snow would melt; the long dead winter would pass away and the world would come alive. Green things would sprout and grow; the sun would ride high and warm; birds would return, singing, to make their nests.

I was reluctant to put my question again, but then I saw that I did not need to. She knew my thoughts.

"As soon as I hear that he has been indicted," she said, "I will keep my share of our bargain. For now I think that you will be safe enough if you stay in your room. I must go downtown. Do not answer the door on any account."

I went upstairs again. For a long time I sat at my window looking down across the treetops to the river. The water ran high; the spring flood had begun. I would have liked to be on the surface of that water, ever flowing, gliding down to the sea, going away. Soon, I thought. Soon she will give them to me and I will be gone. I will have them. I will have won.

In order to feel less confined I had left the door of my room ajar, and so I heard her when, late in the afternoon, she came back. With great caution I walked out to the balustrade and listened. She was alone. I saw her standing in the entrance hall, not yet having removed her hat and coat, standing quite still, looking at . . . what? I could not see. The object of her vision lay beyond—beneath—my own.

It seemed to me at that moment that I gazed upon a stranger: I had never seen this woman. She frightened me. Who was she? What had she to do with me? Why was my life bound in some inexplicable way to hers? (For I knew that it was, although I could not just then remember why.) She seemed, standing there so still, a figure of infinite menace. I did not know who she was, or why she had come to this house. I knew only that I needed her in some way, that she had something that I desperately wanted, that I must get it from her now—this moment—and then get away. Why did she not move? What did she see? What new machination stirred in her brain? It seemed intolerable that I must be at her mercy—this drab, dull, silent woman.

Suddenly, irritated beyond endurance, I spoke her name. She started; she looked up at me. I did not pause to notice the expression on her face. I hurried down the stairs, almost stumbling in my need to get close to her. I paused at the last step. I was aware that I was breathing hard, that my throat was tight, that my voice, when it came, would not be my own.

She smiled at me, but I would not be put off.

"Now," I said.

"What's the matter? You look—"

"Never mind how I look. Give them to me." What? Ah—yes.

She had begun to remove her coat. She paused and looked at me with some concern.

"But it is too soon. I explained to you—"

"Never mind that. I want them now. I have waited too long. You promised them to me."

Someone was speaking very loud: His voice reverberated in my head.

She slipped out of her coat, removed her hat, and went to hang them on the mirrored coat rack in the vestibule. When she returned, her face was composed. She spoke to me calmly, as if I were a child in a temper. Insufferable!

"You remember our agreement. We dare not act too soon."

"I remember nothing but that you have promised and promised and continually put me off with your promises."

"You will ruin everything if you push too hard. They have only just arrested him today—"

223

"Damn them! Damn *you!*" A terrible excitement had mounted in my brain. I felt as if I must explode—as if I must fly at her and seize her by the throat and force—literally throttle—her into submission.

She understood my condition; she acted swiftly to pacify me. With no further word she took a lamp from a side table and opened the parlor door. I followed her in. I did not mind. Something—what?—had happened in this place, but no matter. I had no time now to think of it. The room was dim and cold. The drapes were drawn; ashes lay deep in the grate. I followed her in and from both habit and caution shut the door behind me. I felt as though I had entered a tomb where lay all my dead desires.

She set the lamp on the table, lit it with a match from the mantel, and turned down the wick so that the room was hardly brighter than before. I stood near the door; my body shook with excitement, my hands flexed restlessly, helplessly; my mouth was dry and sour. Silently I spoke to her; silently I willed her to obey me.

She responded as if I had said the words aloud. She stood at the table, the light of the lamp making a harsh mask of her face, and prepared to deal with me.

"If you take them now, you must not tell anyone that you have them."

Silently I assented.

"You will ruin us both if anyone hears you speak of them—or where you got them."

I understood all this. Get on with it!

"Can I not persuade you to wait a little while longer? A few days . . . a week—"

"Now. Give them to me."

With a slight downward movement of her shoulders—a kind of inner collapse—she turned away and knelt before the bookcase. I stood very still, not wanting to distract her.

Now that it had finally come—after all my effort, all my waiting—this moment seemed to be occurring in a dream, and I—the dreamer—feared to awake too soon.

Her hands pressed at the carved panel. It responded to her touch; it slid smoothly across the grooves to reveal the hidden space. I held my breath. She worked in shadow, untouched by the golden circle of the lamp. I strained to see. She reached inside. I saw her arm move as she searched. For an endless moment—a few seconds only—she stayed so. Then she withdrew her hand. She crouched by the bookcase, her head bent, her shoulders hunched in the very image of defeat. The clock on the mantel, unwound, had long since fallen silent; the sound in my ears was the frantic pounding of my overburdened heart.

At last she stood up. She looked at me, but in the gloom I could not see the expression in her eyes.

"I am sorry," she said. Her voice came from a great distance.

Sorry! "Give them to me," I said.

"I cannot. They are not here."

"Give them to me."

"I was sure that she had hidden them here. She must have taken them out—"

"Give them to me!"

"Sometime since you came. She must have put them somewhere else. She was always secretive—"

I did not understand. She had promised them to me. Why now did she refuse?

Swiftly I went to the bookcase. She stepped out of my way; she looked frightened. I knelt and searched. Nothing. On the shelves then—hidden behind the volumes. I began to tear out the books, I threw them on the floor, I felt my rising panic. The bottom shelf, the middle two, the top— Nothing. No envelope stuffed with papers, no packet carefully tied. Behind the bookcase itself then. Roughly I pulled it away from the wall. The light did not penetrate there, I had to get down to examine the dusty space with my hands. As I bent my shoulder hit the shelves. They toppled over onto the pile of books. No matter—I did not care. Nothing lay behind them. Nothing!

I stood up. My desire—my urgency—permitted no delay. In three steps I was upon her. I seized her arm.

"Where have you put them?"

"Nowhere!"

She tried to break away but I would not let her go. I did not care how frightened she was. I was frightened myself—terrified at losing them, at what I might do to get them—ah, at what I had done already! But not in vain—no, never! I would have them!

"Get them for me!"

"But—I don't know where she put them! I swear to you—"

She cried out in pain then, and merely as an automatic reaction I loosened my grip. Before I was aware of what she did, she had wrenched free. She seized the poker—ah, how quick she moved!—and, thus armed, took a threatening stance between me and the door.

"Now," she said, "You may search the room. Go on—I will not stop you. Look anywhere you like. Do not hurry—there is plenty of time. But never—do you hear me?—never touch me again. Do as you please but never touch me. Do you understand?"

We faced each other across the distance. There was no way, it seemed, that I could defeat her. Only by getting what I sought, and then getting free, could I hope to win. Getting free was no problem—I could go through the parlor window if necessary—but the letters—*his* precious words!—ah, that was the difficulty! *Where* had she put them?

I obeyed her. I began to search the room: the escritoire, the sofa, the chairs, feeling the soft stuffing for the shape of the bound packet. I tore off the piano's shawl and lifted the lid over the strings. I felt for hidden panels in the wall, around the fireplace—nothing! I examined everything in the room with no result. I do not know how long I searched. In the end I got down on my hands and knees and crawled around the floor, feeling for loose boards which might conceal a hiding place. Nothing!

She watched me. She held the poker. Whenever I came near to her, her grip seemed to tighten, she seemed to gird herself for open physical combat. She did me an injustice—I wanted no pugilistic contest; I wanted only what was rightfully mine. Those papers were mine. I had earned them well! Ah, where were they?

At last I gave up. I turned to her, I admitted my defeat.

"The attic, then?" she said. "The cellar? You may even search the bedrooms if you like—*her* room. I will not stop you."

Why—when this was the chance I had longed for—why did her words discourage me? She spoke with a curious indecisiveness. Her voice held no promise, no hope. She was, it seemed, as ignorant as I as to their whereabouts. I did not believe it. She knew—I was sure she knew—and she delighted in tormenting me. She had used me—very badly! Now she would not settle our account; she would not give me what she owed. Damn her! I *would* find them!

I rushed past her, aware as I did so that she was alarmed at my approach. I ran upstairs. A back stairway near my room led to the attic. I stumbled in the darkness, cursing my stupidity in forgetting a light. I stopped; I must go back, it seemed, and beg a lamp. I stood halfway up the attic stairs, strengthening myself for that effort, damning my impetuousness.

But no—I did not need to go back. I heard her footstep in the hall; I saw the first faint illumination from her lamp. I waited. She appeared below, looking up, wary, not sure, perhaps, of what she might find. Although the lamp was fairly large, she held it with one hand.

"Go on," she said. "I will bring up the light."

I went ahead. The attic was filled—overflowing. But of course I had visited it before. That occasion had been staged to deceive me. Trunks, cases, tall cabinets, looming, discarded furniture draped in white shrouds, odd pieces—a dress form, a sewing machine, piles of books and papers—my papers?

She put the lamp on a leather trunk and stood quite still beside it. I began my search. I started with a stack of boxes containing periodicals, but there was nothing; it was too obvious, dear Heaven, but these women were a pair of packrats! Was there nothing that they had not kept? Next I attacked the crates—old china, small discarded household utensils, lamps, bric-a-brac of all kinds. But not what I sought! Not a scrap!

I turned to the trunks. Two of them were unlocked. They contained clothing—men's clothing. The late Mr. Richmond's, no doubt. Two more were locked. I felt a momentary surge of hope. Locked! Enormously encouraging! Yes—very good! No place more likely than a locked trunk!

There were, it seemed, no keys. I looked about me for a likely tool. The lamp, pouring its light on the jumble of a lifetime, formed more shadow than illumination. There was a small dark thing on the cabinet of the sewing machine. Yes—an old iron. I took it; my spirits rose as I felt the heavy weight of it.

She moved away from me. She need not have worried. My thoughts were concentrated on the lock.

I smashed at the metal clasp. It fell off. I lifted the lid. Inside: one dress. It seemed to be pale blue. As I lifted it to see what lay below, a clump of dry twigs which had been concealed in its folds fell out at my feet.

A sigh—a small, shocked sound—escaped her. She came near. She put out her hand. Her fingers touched the cloth. Momentarily deflected from my search, I held it for her; I felt like a shopkeeper's assistant.

"I have never seen this," she said. Her voice was flat, devoid of feeling. "I asked her about it once, when I—when it seemed that I might need such a dress. I asked her if I could wear it. I said that it was my dearest wish to wear it. I did not want a new one—no! I was young, stupidly sentimental. I thought that my request would make her happy. I was wrong. She did not speak to me for a week. And by the end of that time—" Her voice failed. Her hand dropped to her side. "By the end of that time I no longer needed it. She had sent him away."

"If he consented to go—" What? I turned away from her, I lowered my arms. The dress crumpled to the floor. I lacked the time—the wit—to formulate a tactful reply, to consider what unhappy memories my discovery might have aroused. I felt around the bottom of the trunk, I checked its dimensions both outside and in, and then, satisfied that it concealed nothing more, I folded the dress and laid it away. She stood beside me; she watched me. I glanced at her face. I could not read its expression. Poor daughter!

Gently I closed the trunk's lid. I lifted the iron, preparing to make the assault on the second lock. I realized that I had been distracted from my purpose. The knowledge frightened me. I could not allow myself to flag, to fail—not now, not when I had the license to succeed!

And yet—and yet——something stayed my hand. I could not lift the iron to make the blow. It was as if I knew— *knew*—that some other sound must come—some other sound that took precedence, as it were, over the clash of metal striking metal, the sound of the shattering lock.

I held my breath. I strained to hear. So intent was I on what I knew must come that I was no longer even aware of my companion—my wardress—standing beside me. I listened.

And then I heard.

Like the cry of a poor lost soul entombed before its time—like the wail of the banshee keening its awful news of impending death—like my own heart weeping for what I had done, what I had lost—listen! Softly beginning, louder and louder it rose, wilder and more insistent, rising and falling, a dreadful lamentation which filled my ears and paralyzed my hand and struck cold terror into my soul— ah, listen!

I heard the crash of the iron as I dropped it. I heard her speak to me, but I could not understand what she said. The sound possessed me—maddened me—where was it? Rising and falling, rising and falling, coming close, coming here—! No human ever made such a sound. No human—

And then I knew.

Do you understand? This voice—this cry from beyond the grave—was not her voice. No! She was dead, she lay quiet in her tomb, she would not walk to persecute me! No! She was at peace now, with him. Ah, no—this sound upon me now was a far more fearsome thing!

The daughter had told me it was dead. I had the scars on my hands still. I had struggled mightily, but in the end

I had won. I was so very sure—listen! It is here—with me! Ah, help me—!

I escaped. I ran to the narrow stairs, I stumbled down, I ran out into the second floor hall. At once I realized my mistake, for the sound was louder now, more insistent, calling to me—yes! That was it! I must follow it, I must go where it summoned me! And then I would find what I sought—yes!

I forced myself to be still. No light penetrated from the attic; no light shone from the rooms below. All was black—pitch-dark. The sound filled my ears, it throbbed inside my head. Rising and falling, rising and falling— Which way?

My feet moved independent of my will. Helpless, unable to resist, I shuffled toward the source of that unearthly summons. I knew where it led me—yes! Darkness enveloped me, I gasped for air, I suffocated in that awful black. And yet I went on, my hand found the knob, I opened the door—her door!—my head near burst with the noise— Here it was! Yes!—and here they were, my precious papers, hidden here in her own room and guarded by the spirit of the beast who had so savagely clawed me, the beast whom I had killed!

A faint illumination through the window showed the presence of the waning moon. I could see a little—not the beast, no, although its cry rose to cacophony here—but the outlines of the room, the bulk of desk and table and bed, those I saw, and those were sufficient to my need. I attacked them. I tore out the drawers of the desk, recklessly, indiscriminately; I flung out every paper, every notebook and diary, every small neat pile of receipts. Nothing! Louder and louder—ah, cry on, beast, that I may know I am near! I left the desk. I staggered toward the bed. I saw now that a shawl-draped trunk stood between it and the wall. I lunged at it—yes! Screech thy message, guide my hand, louder and louder from the blackness of my soul sing thy awful dirge—!

I tore off the cloth. There was no lock. I wrenched up the lid, I thrust down my hand, I felt—

Ah, no! The scream tore from my throat. *No!* It cannot be! He is dead—far away—locked safe in his coffin in Baltimore! He is there—I knew, I *knew* that he slept peacefully there, undisturbed—!

She had got his suit, the daughter said. But surely not his bones as well! No—no—there must be some mistake! He lies in his grave, he cannot be here with me now!

Fleshless ribs rattled under my trembling fingers. White shapes gleamed from the depths of the trunk; a gaping skull grinned up at me, black empty sockets whose eyes once had seen—what? *Her?*

I thought just then that the thing would move, that it would rise up, that with a dreadful clattering it would come at me, the long fingers seize my throat—

No—do not! Lie still! *Stay—*!

I do not want *you!* Has she kept you here to guard the treasure—the prize which I have so remorselessly pursued?

Who are you?

I was aware of the glimmer of the lamp behind me. I turned—too late! I had a glimpse of her face—of her murderous fury, her mask of hate— and then the iron firestick crashed down on my head and I saw no more.

26

I HAVE BEEN alone since that night. I never see her now. She leaves my meals on a tray. My sole companion is the Raven.

Evil bird! It watches me. I feel its eyes. Several times I have politely asked it to look away. Still it watches. It cannot move, of course—it is a prize example of the taxidermist's art, but even taxidermists cannot give movement to their subjects. So I have the advantage. I can get about. I can walk from window to bed, from bed to window. I do—I walk constantly, under its eye.

Once I tried to turn its face to the wall. No use: I felt compelled—I cannot explain it–to put it facing me again. One must, after all, have some friend: The Raven is mine. It sits on the bureau, silent, immobile, watching.

Of course I must get away. I understand that. But I am cautious. I know that she expects me to escape; I know that she waits for me with her weapon. The moment I step outside this door she will attack me again. It is too great a risk for me. I must wait. I must find a time when she has abandoned her vigil.

Someone else once tried to escape this house. I have seen him. He lies in a trunk. I must be careful or I will lie with him.

How dreadful to be so confined.

I must not think of it.

She fears that I will go to the police. She is wrong. Why should I? I will vanish from her life. She will never hear from me again. I must find a way to make her understand. If only we could talk together! We used to talk. I remember. She seemed fond of me once. Why, now, does she hate me? I feel her hatred very strongly. It permeates the house; its malevolence shrivels my spirit and fogs my brain. I cannot think clearly. Every time I consider my condition—my fate—I become confused. How did I come here? Why? What keeps me?

I do not like to worry over these things, and so I put them out of my mind. The Raven knows; soon it will tell me. Until then I will be calm. I will wait. I will watch for my chance to escape. Meanwhile the Raven will protect me. I think of it as a guardian. But it is a jealous bird. It would be angry if I tried to abandon it. Perhaps, then, it would fly at me. I am sure that it cannot move, but anything is possible. Now. So I am very careful. I speak to it with the greatest respect.

I have said that I am alone. But I have seen someone else in this room. He is elusive—a spirit only. I caught a glimpse of his face yesterday as I passed the mirror. He is a wild man. I must be careful of him. I must think of some way to defend myself if he returns.

And yet he had a beautiful moustache. Perhaps he will give me the name of his barber.

The Raven saw him, too.

She has taken all my money.

I must get away.

27

MY CHANCE CAME. I took it.

It happened this way: Always when she brought my tray she went back along the hall and into her room and stayed there behind the door. My hearing had become very sharp. I knew always, from the sound of her footsteps, what she did, where she went.

Always after I had eaten and put the tray outside my door again, she came to take it away. But she never went to the kitchen. Her footsteps (how clearly I heard them!) stopped always at the dining room. Then they came back as she resumed her vigil behind her door.

But this day—evening, rather—was different. She did not return; she stayed downstairs. I listened: nothing. Where had she gone? Did she wait for me there, crouched by the staircase, ready to fly out and strike me as I crept away?

I had to try.

I picked up my razor, I stepped into the hall. Silently I walked to the head of the stairs. Nothing—darkness, total silence. Except— For a moment I held my breath. What had I heard?

A strange sound, an unaccustomed sound.

Like the rustling of a skirt, and yet somehow not that—a sharper sound.

Never mind.

Carefully, silently I descended. Nothing. I paused at the last step. So acute had my hearing become that I would have known at once had anyone stood waiting to seize me in the darkness.

There was no one. I was sure of it.

I made my way to the front door. I reached it—opened it—I stepped out onto the porch.

A black night—no moon, the stars obscured by heavy clouds. Very cold. No matter. Soon I would run, I would warm myself. I took a deep breath. The fresh air hurt my lungs.

I made my way down the drive, setting my feet carefully on the crushed stones. As I went I struggled to restrain myself. I wanted to run—to escape quickly. Running was out of the question until I reached the road—I dared not risk the noise. But as I went I looked back over my shoulder, for I was sure—I *felt*—that someone followed me. I saw nothing, and yet I knew that someone came. I heard nothing except my painful breath, the pounding of my heart——and yet—what was that sound?

Hurry.

I reached the gate, I came out onto the road. Hurry. I forced myself to continue walking. Not until I reached the next house, some distance down the road, did I begin to run.

238

And then I ran—furiously! Someone followed me; I was sure of it, although I could not see him—*her?*—as I looked back. I stumbled, I fell, I picked myself up. I felt blood trickle from my forehead.

I ran. I reached the crest of the hill, I saw the lights of the city below. The huge bulks of the factory buildings were brightly illuminated. Street lights outlined the thoroughfares. Someone there would help me; surely someone there would save me from my pursuers.

I ran. Down the hill, across a bridge, into the city. I heard a factory whistle as I went.

Where? Who could help me? My lungs burned, my heart near burst, my trembling legs were hardly strong enough to carry me—where?

I trotted down a street of shops. Anxiously I scanned the faces of passers-by. Old, young, men, women, tired-looking, most of them, hurrying home, here and there a lively eye. No one seemed to notice me. No one seemed disposed to stop, to offer kind assistance. Please—!

I needed to calm myself. I must not make a scene, I thought. Despite my fear of those who followed me, I forced myself to slow, to walk. I felt faint. Now, for the first time, I suffered from the cold. Stupid! I should have taken my hat, my greatcoat.

I paused. I leaned against the bright display of a jeweler's window. Who could help me?

I saw a policeman walking by. He threw me a curious glance. No—no, that was no good at all. I must not become involved with the police.

I moved on. I tried to lose myself in the crowd. People everywhere—who could help me? No one knew me here—except—yes! Of course!

I thought I remembered the way. I turned a corner—yes—a few blocks down, I had walked this very street my first day here. I knew now where I was. I knew now where I could find help. I hurried on.

The lobby was crowded; no one looked at me as I went in. Every breath I drew tore at my lungs, I could not focus my eyes for the pounding in my head.

I approached the desk. The clerk was unfamiliar—not the man with whom I had dealt. He was busy with a customer; he did not see me. I turned away.

The dining room was filled. I approached it; I stood at the door. No one noticed me. I looked at the noisy crowd—eating, talking, gesticulating—happy faces, satisfied faces, gorging, masticating, calling to the racing waiters, a great clatter and hum, very warm under the bright electric lamps. The sight mesmerized me. I felt that I had come here from another world. I was not hungry, not a bit, but suddenly I longed to enter that room, to sit with someone, to talk, to share the company of another human being. Ah, how lonely I was!

Then I saw him. He sat with someone else—a woman. He was partly turned away from me so that at first I was not sure, but then he moved his head and I saw his pink, fleshy face. Relief flooded my soul. I went in.

At first he pretended not to see me. He was telling a long story to the woman; he did not want an interruption. At last, forced to rudeness by my desperation, I sat down. Then, of course, he had to acknowledge me. He broke off in the middle of a sentence, he looked up, annoyed.

I reminded him of our dinner together some weeks ago. I asked him if, in memory of that pleasant occasion, he could do me a service.

He shook his head. He told me that he did not recollect our acquaintance. His tone was surly. Obviously he was not a gentleman. But of course I had known that. I did not care.

I asked, very politely, although I was trembling—frantic—with fear—I asked him if he would step outside for a moment. There was something extremely important, I said, that I had to tell him.

I saw in his eyes the first faint shadow of alarm. It was not my intention to alarm him. I spoke again, more rapidly, trying to reassure him. I wanted nothing, I said, but to speak to him privately for a moment.

I watched him struggle with himself. Please, I said, I would not ask you if it were not so terribly urgent—

At last he got up, he excused himself to his companion, he walked out and I followed. He paused in the lobby and turned to me, exasperated, but I touched his arm and motioned him on. I wanted to be outside; I did not like to speak in the lobby, where we might be overheard. I did not know exactly where my enemy was. He—*she*—might be anywhere; I must not risk being caught. Outside on the hotel porch we would be alone; no one could hear us there above the noise of the traffic in the street.

We stood well away from the door. I was very nervous; I could not meet his eyes. I explained my difficulty to him. He did not at first appear to comprehend. I explained again. The main thing, of course, was my appearance: the moustache was quite distinctive. I had to get rid of it—to shave it off. But my hands trembled so that I feared to use the razor myself. I asked him if he could do me that service—in only a few moments' time, I said, my appearance could be completely transformed. Then I might have a chance to get away. And if he could lend me the price of a train ticket—? I swore to him that I would make good the debt, I told him my name—my real name—and I promised not only to repay him but to give him a generous reward as well. It seemed impossible that he would refuse to help me, and yet he did not reply; he gave no word of encouragement, he stood uneasy, waiting to escape, unmoved by my plea. I held out the razor to him, but he did not take it.

Damn him! Could he not see the logic of what I said? Of course I had to disguise myself to get away safely; of course I had to beg money when all my own had been taken from me! But no—he did not understand.

I realized then that I must explain my predicament more fully. I began with the night of my arrival—the night I had met him, although he denied it. I spoke rapidly; time was everything; soon my escape would be discovered. I had a few moments only—

He began to back away from me. There was a curious expression on his face—a reflection of my own fear. No—I begged him—please stay, hear me out, you must help me. I am hunted, they will find me, they will take me back to that house, they will force me to look at certain paintings in an upstairs room, they will show me something in a trunk—ah, but he did not know about the Raven! How then could he understand?

I explained to him, I warned him. It is a fearsome bird, I said; never let it come near you.

I saw that at last my my words had begun to take effect. He was properly frightened then! Sensible man!

Yes, I said, and so of course you see my difficulty, for if that bird sees me as I am now it will recognize me at once, and so of course you see my difficulty for I must disguise myself but I cannot do it alone—

A hand touched my arm. I very nearly cried out, but I managed to control myself. One does not make a scene in public.

I turned. In the harsh illumination of the electric lamps I saw her.

Surprisingly she smiled. She, too, knew the importance

242

of keeping up appearances. Behind her stood two rough-looking men. They did not smile.

Of course I could have broken away; I could have run had I had any sanctuary. Had I had the strength to face a public trial—public humiliation, exposure to the world of my private obsession so miserably thwarted—

As it was, I gave up without a struggle. They led me away to a hired carriage. My friend stood at the hotel door and watched us go. I glimpsed him from the carriage window as we went. I was surprised. I had not thought him capable of an expression of such generous pity.

A shadow fell across his face and swiftly passed away again. I need not tell you what it was. I heard its triumphant cry, and then all was obliterated by the sound of my own uncontrollable weeping.

I had been right—without the moustache they never would have found me.

28

IT WATCHES ME.

It never moves and still it watches me.

It never moves, and yet—

What did I hear last night?

A tapping, a rapping—at my window!

Ah, fearsome bird! You cannot frighten me now!

Tap away—I am beyond fear.

And yet—what was that noise?

The bird is here with me. Was it trying to escape?

I pull the covers over my head.

In the morning—but how do I know that day has come? My room is dark, no light shines through the window.

Why?

The problem vexes me. I rise from my bed to investigate.

A tapping, a rapping—but see! I had heard it, after all! I *had* heard—

Strange! Did he not compose this tale many years ago? What was the name of his unfortunate character? Yes—Fortunato. Delicious! Or was Montresor the truly unfortunate one? I cannot remember.

But I remember clearly enough the sensation which gripped me as I read. Suffocation—yes!—although the focus of the plot was on the perpetrator of the horrible deed rather than his victim. I suffered mightily reading that story. It haunts me still.

How dreadful to be walled up alive.

I must not think of it or I will go mad.

I must investigate the sound. I am very weak; I can hardly move, but I must make my way across the room—

Yes. I was right. Here, you see, was my window. It afforded, as I recollect, a fine view of the river.

They have boarded it over from the outside.

I can see nothing.

I must not think of it.

They do not want me to escape again.

They?

29

THE DOOR, too, is boarded over.

Hammering, hammering—I knew what they did; they could not deceive me. I shouted at them but they did not answer.

When they had finished—yesterday?—they went away. She has gone, too.

Since then I have heard no sound. No sound, that is, from without this room.

Inside—yes—here with me—I hear a great deal. I hear rapping and tapping, I hear a curious high-pitched laugh, I hear a long low sobbing through the night. I think it is night; I cannot tell.

She has gone away.

I am alone with the bird.

It watches me.

30

WHAT IS THE TIME?

Late, late—I must hurry.

I have begun to compose a tale.

Where is Muddie? Often she sat with him through the night as he worked. I wish she were here with me now.

I am very tired. The tale is complex; I cannot remember the beginning.

I cannot remember why I came to this house.

If I write it out, I will find the proper motivation for my narrator. It is important that he have a reason for his actions.

Is it not?

Once they told him that he was a genius.

He never had enough to eat.

Understand me: